OTHER WORKS BY JEAN-PHILIPPE TOUSSAINT
IN ENGLISH TRANSLATION

THE BATHROOM

MONSIEUR

CAMERA

TELEVISION

MAKING LOVE

Running Away

Originally published in French as *Fuir* by Les Éditions de Minuit, 2005

First English translation, 2009

Library of Congress Cataloging-in-Publication Data

Toussaint, Jean-Philippe.
[Fuir. English]
Running away / Jean-Philippe Toussaint ; translated by Matthew B. Smith. -- 1st English translation.
p. cm.
ISBN 978-1-56478-567-1 (pbk. : alk. paper)
I. Smith, Matthew B. II. Title.
PQ2680.O86F8513 2009
843'.914--dc22
2009021379

Partially funded by a grant from the Illinois Arts Council, a state agency, and by the University of Illinois at Urbana-Champaign

www.dalkeyarchive.com

Cover: design and composition by Danielle Dutton, illustration by Nicholas Motte
Printed on permanent/durable acid-free paper and bound in the United States of America

Running Away

Jean-Philippe Toussaint
Translated by Matthew B. Smith

Dalkey Archive Press
Champaign & London

summer

Would it ever end with Marie? The summer before we broke up I spent a few weeks in Shanghai, but it wasn't really a business trip, more a pleasure junket, even if Marie had given me a sort of mission (but I don't feel like going into details). The day I arrived in Shanghai, Zhang Xiangzhi, a business associate of Marie's, was there to meet me at the airport. I'd only seen him once before, in Paris, at Marie's office, but I recognized him immediately, he was talking to a uniformed police officer just past customs. He had to be in his forties, round cheeks, facial features swollen, smooth, copper-colored skin, and he wore very dark sunglasses that seemed too big for his small face. We were waiting at the edge of the baggage carousel for my bag and we'd hardly exchanged a few words in broken English before he handed me a cell phone. *Present for you*, he told me, which plunged me into a state of extreme bewilderment. I didn't really understand why he felt the need to give me a cell phone, a used cell phone, rather ugly, dull gray, without packaging or instructions. To keep an eye on me, be able to locate me at any time, watch my every move? I don't know. I followed him silently through the airport terminal, and I felt a sense of unease, heightened by jet lag and the tension that comes with arriving in an unknown city.

On exiting the airport, Zhang Xiangzhi made a quick gesture with his hand and a shiny new gray Mercedes slowly rolled up to us. He got in behind the wheel, sending the driver, a young guy with a fluid, scarcely noticeable presence, to the back seat after having placed my bag in the trunk. Seated at the wheel, Zhang Xiangzhi invited me to join him in the front, and I sat beside him on a comfortable, cream-leather seat with armrests and a new-car scent while he tried to adjust the air conditioning, which, after fiddling with a digital touch pad, began humming softly in the vehicle. I handed him the manila envelope that Marie had asked me to give him (which contained twenty-five thousand dollars cash). He opened it, thumbed quickly through the bundles to count the bills, then resealed the envelope before putting it in his back pocket. He fastened his seat belt and we left the airport slowly to get on the freeway in the direction of Shanghai. We didn't say a word, he didn't speak

French and his English was poor. He wore a gray short-sleeved shirt and a small gold chain with a pendant in the shape of a stylized claw or dragon's talon around his neck. I still had the cell phone he had given me, it was on my lap, I didn't know what to do with it or why it had even been offered to me in the first place (just a Welcome to China gift?). I was aware of the fact that Zhang Xiangzhi had been overseeing Marie's real-estate investments in China for a few years now, some possibly dishonest and illicit activities, renting out and selling commercial leases, purchasing building space in rundown areas, the whole thing probably tainted by corruption and all sorts of clandestine exchanges of money. Since her first bouts of success in Asia, in Korea and Japan, Marie had set up shop in Hong Kong and Beijing and had been hoping to acquire new storefronts in Shanghai and in the south of China, with plans underway to open branches in Shenzhen and Guangzhou. For the time being, however, I hadn't heard anything about Zhang Xiangzhi being involved in organized crime.

On arriving at the Hansen Hotel, where a room had been reserved for me, Zhang Xiangzhi parked the Mercedes in the hotel's private interior courtyard and went to grab my bag from the trunk before ushering me all the way to the front desk. He hadn't been involved in any way with reserving the room, which was done from Paris by a travel agency (a one-week, fully planned "escapade" with hotel and flight included, to which I added an extra week of vacation for my own enjoyment), but now he was seeing to everything, having me step aside as he took care of the arrangements. He had me wait on a couch while he went alone to the front desk to check me in. I sat there waiting in the lobby, next to a depressing display of dusty plants withering in flowerpots, and I watched him listlessly as he filled out my registration information. At one point he walked over to me, hurried, concerned, his hand reaching out anxiously, to ask me for my passport. He walked back to the front desk and I kept an eye on my passport, watching it with some concern as it passed from hand to hand, worried that I might see it spirited out of the hands of one of the numerous employees shuffling behind the counter. After a few more minutes of waiting, Zhang Xiangzhi came back over to me with the magnetic key card for my room. It was enclosed in a red and white case adorned with carefully formed Chinese characters, but he didn't give it to me, he kept it in his hand. He grabbed my bag and invited me to follow him, and we headed to the elevators to go up to my room.

It was a three-star hotel, clean and quiet, we didn't see a single person on our floor, I followed Zhang Xiangzhi down a long deserted hall, an abandoned housekeeping cart blocked our way. Zhang Xiangzhi slid the magnetic card through the lock and we entered my room (very dark, the curtains were drawn). I fiddled with the light at the door but the dimmer switch turned without effect. I tried to turn on the bedside lamp, but there was no electricity in the room. Zhang Xiangzhi pointed at a little receptacle on the wall next to the door in which one was meant to insert the key card in order to turn on the electricity. To demonstrate, he slowly inserted the card into the little slot and all the lights lit up at once, in the closet as well as the bathroom, the air conditioner loudly began to emit cool air, and the bathroom fan turned on. Zhang Xiangzhi went to open the curtains and stood at the window for a moment, pensive, looking at the new Mercedes parked in the courtyard below. Then he turned back around, as if to leave—or so I thought. He sat down in the armchair, crossed his legs, and took out his own cell phone, and, without appearing to be inconvenienced in any way by my presence (I was standing in the middle of the room, exhausted from my trip, I wanted to shower and stretch out on the bed) he began dialing a number, closely following the instructions on a blue phone card that had the letters "IP" written on it, followed by various codes and Chinese characters. He needed to start over a couple of times before getting it right, and then, gesturing emphatically in my direction, he called me over, had me run to his side, so that he could hand me the phone. I didn't know what to say, where to speak, to whom or in what language I would be speaking, before hearing a female voice say *allô*, apparently in French, *allô*, she repeated. *Allô*, I finally said. *Allô*, she said. Our confusion was now complete (I was beginning to feel uneasy). Marie? With his sharp and focused eyes aimed at me, Zhang Xiangzhi was prodding me to talk, assuring me that it was Marie on the line—Marie, Marie, he was repeating while pointing at the phone—and I finally understood that he had dialed Marie's number in Paris (her office number, the only one that he had) and that I was talking to a secretary at the haute-couture house *Let's Go Go Go*. But I didn't feel like talking to Marie right now, not at all, especially in front of Zhang Xiangzhi. Feeling more and more uneasy, I wanted to hang up, but I didn't know which button to push or how to stop the conversation, so I quickly tossed him the phone as though it were white-hot. He hung it up, brusquely snapped it shut, pensive. He retrieved it from his lap, brushed it on the back of his hand as if to dust it off, and leaned forward to hand it to me without leaving his chair. *For you*, he told me, and he explained to me in English that, if I wanted to make a call, I should always use this card, dial 17910, then 2 for instructions in English (1 for Mandarin, if I preferred), the card's number, followed by his

PIN, 4447, then 00 for international, 33 for France, and then the number itself, etc. *Understand?* he asked. I said yes, more or less (maybe not all the details, but I got the gist of it). If I wanted to make a call, I should always use this card—always, he insisted—and, pointing to the room's old landline phone on the bedside table, he shook his finger, saying no forcefully, like an order or command. *No*, he said. *Understand? No. Never. Very expensive,* he said, *very very expensive.*

In the following days, Zhang Xiangzhi called me only once or twice on the cell phone he had given me to see how I was doing and to invite me to lunch. Since my arrival, I had spent most of my time alone in Shanghai, not doing much, not meeting anyone. I'd walk around the city, eating at random times and places, seasoned kidney skewers on street corners, burning hot bowls of noodles in tiny hole-in-the-wall places packed with people, sometimes more elaborate meals in luxurious hotel restaurants, slowly working my way through the menus in deserted kitsch dining halls. In the afternoon, I'd take a nap in my room, not going back out until nightfall when it would get a little cooler. I'd go for a walk in the mild night, lost in thought, strolling alongside the multicolored neon-lit shops of Nanjing Road, indifferent to the noise and constant activity. Drawn to the river, I'd always end up in the Bund, welcomed by its maritime atmosphere and sea breeze. I'd cross through the underground passageway and amble aimlessly along the river, letting my eyes fall upon the row of old European buildings whose green lights, reflected on the wavy water of the Huangpu, projected emerald halos in the night. From the other bank of the river, beyond the flow littered with vegetable waste stagnating in the darkness, beyond the chunks of mud floating on the surface of the water and the algae magically held in place by an invisible undertow, the skyscrapers of Pudong traced a futuristic line in the sky as fateful as the lines that mark our palms, punctuated by the distinctive sphere of the Oriental Pearl, and, further along on the right, as if in retreat, modest and hardly lit up, the discreet majesty of the Jin Mao Tower. Looking out at the water, pensive, I was captivated by the river's dark and wavy surface, and in a state of dreamlike melancholy—as often happens when the thought of love is met with the spectacle of dark water in the night—I was thinking about Marie.

Was it already a lost cause with Marie? And what could I have known about it then?

I hadn't originally planned to go to Beijing during this trip, it was a spontaneous decision to spend a few days there. Zhang

Xiangzhi had called one night inviting me at a moment's notice to an art gallery opening. The exhibition was held on the outskirts of the city, in a former warehouse that now served as a contemporary art space, where a few artists had installed these mobile video installations, projectors attached to metal ceiling shafts, slowly swinging through the emptiness of the dark warehouse, causing projected images to converge on the walls before splitting and spreading apart only to come together and reform again. That's where I met Li Qi. She was sitting on the cement floor, her back against the wall, alone in the room, long black hair and cream leather jacket. I noticed her presence immediately but didn't speak to her until later, next to the refreshments, Australian wines and bottles of Chinese beer stacked on a trestle table also holding various fliers and art catalogues. She had noticed that I wasn't Chinese (her perspicacity amused me—and what makes you think that? I asked her). Your smile, she said, your small trace of a smile (all of this in English, maintaining that same small trace of a smile which came irrepressibly to our lips when we first started talking, set off by nothing in particular and seeming to feed continuously now on what was really rather benign fuel). We had gone to sit down on a bench in a vacant area outside the gallery with two bottles of Tsingtao, then four, then six, then night, unhurriedly, fell, and we were still together, our silhouettes like shadow puppets which couldn't have been more Chinese, lit up intermittently by the shifting play of liquid light, green and red, coming from the moving videos inside the gallery. Sound checks could be heard from the warehouse, and sharp bursts of Chinese heavy metal suddenly filled the calm surroundings of the summer night, causing glass panes to vibrate and sending grasshoppers flying in the warmth of the air. It became difficult to hear one another on the bench and I moved closer to her, but, rather than raising my voice to speak over the music, I continued to talk to her in a low voice, her hair tickling my face, my lips close to her ear, I could smell the scent of her skin, could almost feel the touch of her cheek, and she showed no sign of resistance, sitting still, not making the slightest effort to lean away—I could see her eyes in the dark night staring off into the distance while listening to me—and I understood then that something was beginning to develop between us. She explained to me that she had to go back to Beijing the next day for her work and suggested that I go with her, I could just stay a night or two, nothing would keep me from going back to Shanghai the day after tomorrow, the night train was comfortable and inexpensive—and, in any case, I didn't have anything in particular to do in Shanghai, right? I took a minute to think, not too long, before smiling at her, looking into her eyes to question the exact nature of her offer and its latent—albeit implicit, already pleasurable—amorous innuendos.

I checked out of my hotel in the evening of the day of my departure. I didn't bring any luggage, only a bag with a few toiletries, as well as the cell phone I'd been given, and which never rang (besides, nobody had my number apart from Xiangzhi and Marie). Since I still had a lot of time, I took a bus to the train station rather than take a taxi, and I watched the streets of Shanghai file by through the window in the orange-tinted twilight of sunset.

Li Qi and I had planned to meet in front of the Shanghai railway station, but we might as well have planned to meet "in China": Thousands of people were swarming in every direction, heading toward the subway or bus station entrances, entering and exiting the illuminated glass structure of the station, while, alongside it, hundreds of passengers crowded in the shade against its transparent walls, crouching and still, with a sort of dark and restrained look, farmers and seasonal workers who had just arrived or were waiting for the night train with bags and sacks at their feet, worn, split open, untied, crates and overstuffed cardboard boxes, jute sacks spewing over, bundles, gear, here and there a loosely knotted tarp with pots and portable stoves spilling out. Searching for Li Qi in a stifling heat that smelled like dirty clothes, I felt as though I were the object of countless whispers and furtive glances. An aging homeless women stood by my side without moving, leaning on a large wooden crutch, head held stubbornly high, hunched over with her hand out, eyes infinitely sad. I was beginning to think that Li Qi wouldn't show—it had all been so quick: the night before, we hadn't even really gotten to know each other—when I finally spotted her in the distance, cutting through the crowd to get to me, picking up her pace the last few meters. She grabbed my arm, out of breath, smiling, she was wearing a light, loose-fitting khaki jacket, hardly a jacket, more like a blouse whose opening revealed a tight black undershirt, and, on her neck, I noticed a tiny spark of jade shinning on her naked skin. But, practically at the same time, a few meters behind her, in her wake so to speak, I caught sight of Zhang Xiangzhi, with his black sunglasses, trailing unhurriedly behind her in the night. I didn't understand what was going on, and I was suddenly overcome by a feeling of uneasiness, irritation, and uncertainty. After having greeted me with a smile that seemed ironic, maybe even mocking, as if wanting me to acknowledge the bad trick he had played on me—or the trick I had tried to play on him, which he hadn't fallen for—Zhang Xiangzhi stepped away to make a call on his cell phone. What was he doing here? Had he simply accompanied Li Qi to the train station? There was certainly nothing surprising about the fact that Li Qi and Zhang Xiangzhi knew each other (it was through him that I had met her, after all), but I couldn't understand how he had found out about our trip—and I was even more taken aback when Li Qi informed me that he was coming along with us to Beijing.

We left the train station behind us and began to run (I no longer tried to understand what was happening, so many things had seemed obscure to me since my arrival in China), we ran across a wide boulevard, blinded by the bright headlights of passing cars, and went into an old brick building, where, in the yellow half-light, the pernicious smells of piss and rancid cabbage reigned. Two police officers on watch guarded the door, indifferent and silent, uniformed, clubs attached to their belts. We had hardly stepped into the building when a host of scalpers were on our heels like a swarm of insects, vehement and voluble, trying to sell us black-market train tickets. It was a vast space that resembled an illegal gambling hall, throbbing with activity, with an ancient ticket machine and empty ticket windows, cigarette butts on the floor, crenellated food-containers abandoned on the ground, and globs of humid spit almost everywhere, scattered like starred constellations lighting up the floor tiling with their nacreous glints. Zhang Xiangzhi began to examine the tickets that the scalpers were offering him and followed a little group into the shadow of a pillar. Surrounded by about a dozen scalpers within inches of his face—only his head stuck out of the mass of waving arms and heaving shoulders—he took a giant bundle of faded, rose-colored hundred yuan bills out of his pocket and drew (counting them conspicuously with his thumb) six bills from the bundle, which he handed to a particular scalper. This person, outraged, pushed the bills back violently, gesturing that he couldn't accept such an offer, imitating the act of getting his throat slit with his thumb, and tried to forcibly seize the whole bundle in order to get more out of their negotiations, which were now getting out of control, even on the verge of provoking an accident, brawl, fist fight. Finally, breaking away from the clutches of the group with a single thrust of his shoulder, Zhang Xiangzhi took three more old and crumpled bills out from his shirt pocket, twenty yuan notes, which he added to the six bills of hundred yuan previously offered, and the exchange was made, swift, vulgar, brutal, three Shanghai-Beijing train tickets for six hundred and sixty yuan, cash.

Before entering the train station we had to go through a security checkpoint. I placed my bag on the conveyer belt, and a security guard, seated off to the side, behind glass, meticulously examined its contents on his control screen, observing the black and clear contours of my toilet kit and cell phone, while my undergarments, more ethereal, grayish, and seemingly immaterial, seemed to float along a clothes line invisible to the surface of the screen, irradiated socks and underwear in limbo. Having passed through the security checkpoint, we reached the Shanghai-Beijing train waiting area, which was already packed, and we forcefully worked our way through the crowd toward a row of chain-blocked turnstiles, guarded by an army of security guards. Wasting no time in turning back around, Zhang Xiangzhi left to find newspapers and drinks for the trip, threading his way back through the crowd, stepping over bags and suitcases scattered on the floor. For the first time since the previous night, I found myself alone with Li Qi. I was looking at her face amid the crowd, still and pensive, and I was wondering why she had invited me to come with her on this trip, while, at the same time, inviting Zhang Xiangzhi to accompany us. Because it was she who had spoken to him about it—how, otherwise, could he have known? I became even more concerned when Li Qi, rather reserved around me up till now, took advantage of Zhang Xiangzhi's absence to open up her wheeled suitcase and take out a little gift for me. She handed it to me, eyes lowered, with visible emotion. I smiled at her, not knowing what to say. I was holding her gift in my hand, without opening it, and, to put an end to our mutual discomfort, I moved close to her and clumsily kissed her on the cheek, with visible timidity, and my discomfort became even more acute as our eyes briefly met and our lips grazed each other, not so fortuitously as one might think.

The night train was stopped at the platform at the Shanghai railway station, and we walked along the long, convex-shaped sleeping cars through whose windows we could make out rows of bunks in the illuminated compartments. Zhang Xiangzhi, leading the way, handed the tickets to the ticket collector, a young lady in a uniform wearing a hat with golden braids, who was standing in front of the door. She spent a long time verifying our IDs, turning and looking at our passports from different angles, attentively examining my visa, then she punched the tickets and checked some numbers on her security sheet before letting us board the train. Moving with difficulty down the aisle to reach our seats, we passed people drinking tea in their bunks, heads bent under the canopy of the midlevel bunk or nested in the top one, reading newspapers, stockinged feet crossed comfortably on fluffy bed pads. A metal food cart filled with drinks and instant soup was held up in traffic in the middle of the aisle, the young employee, hatless and wearing a badge, was making a commotion as she tried to get through, turning around to solicit the ticket inspector's attention. In the aisle, a young man, sleeves rolled up, was standing on a small ladder, hauling up large bags and suitcases, shoving them in overhead baggage compartments, all while being watched by an old couple in blue cotton pajamas. We reached our compartment, and I went to wait in the vestibule for our departure. The train began to move forward through the green half-light of the platform, and, leaning out the window, I looked into a darkness softened by the white and wan light of lampposts glowing in the night.

A few minutes after departure, as we walked through the train in search of the dining car, I noticed that one of the vestibule doors had been broken, from the looks of it only a short time ago, glass shards were scattered all over the floor and traces of dried blood formed a constellation on the door, with one large spot, centrally located, and thousands of dried droplets around it, miniscule, sequined, of a reddish-brown color. There was nothing more than a loosely attached plastic sheet, held only by a strand of adhesive tape and flapping around wildly as air currents rushed through the windowless door, replacing the broken pane. There were no traces of a fight or accident, no clues as to what might have happened. I stopped for a moment in front of this mysterious bloodstain, and Li Qi lingered there with me. Then, during this pause, our shoulders touched, almost intentionally brushed up against one another, as if each seeking this physical contact—it was impossible that it was entirely accidental, our eyes met again and I knew then without any doubt that she was also conscious of this secret contact, which, like a sketch of what was to come, bore within it the promise of a more comprehensive embrace, whose realization, though presently deferred, wouldn't take long to effect.

We sat down in the dining car and ordered a few dishes: skewers, ginger pork, fried noodles. The tablecloth was stained with brown tea spills and sauce from an earlier meal, ashes piled over the edges of tea saucers filled with cigarette butts. Li Qi ate in silence, raising her head from time to time to flash me a brief and complicit look, which Zhang Xiangzhi would always fail to notice. In the back of the dining car, near the kitchen, a small crowd had formed around a young shirtless Chinese man slumped over on a bench, pressing a balled-up bloody handkerchief against the arch of his eyebrow. He looked weak; his white, blood-stained shirt had been taken off and placed on the table amid the remains of a meal, rolled into a ball on the tablecloth, wrinkled, torn, a sleeve bathing in sauce. Seated across from him, two uniformed police officers wearing helmets were interrogating him with countless questions, forcefully grabbing his arm from time to time to make him answer. But the young guy seemed to have no strength, was on the verge of passing out, sweating heavily, drool hanging from his mouth, his forehead and neck moist, sweat mixing with streams of dried blood on his cheeks and chest, crusting up around his nipples. A train conductor took him by the arm and he was then ushered into the hall by the police officers through a whispering and scattered crowd, among which a young girl, worked-up, hair disheveled, was brandishing a twisted red sneaker in the middle of the mêlée and screaming curses, threatening to kick the young guy's face in with her heel.

We had finished eating, empty beer cans were piling up in front of us on the dirty tablecloth. I was looking out the window, trying to see anything out in the darkness we were traveling through, plains or rice fields, in the zone of indistinct shadow that I knew to be the Chinese countryside. I had no idea where we could be, how far north in mainland China, near what city, and, had I known, I would at least have been able to orient myself in some way, Nantong, Lianyungang, Qingdao, I couldn't see the slightest sign of the sea on the horizon, no sand dunes or port constructions, warehouses, or dockyards in the night. A stewardess, walking slowly down the aisle of the somnolent train, wearing a white apron and a small cloth hat, cleared tables one after another with weary gestures, picking up dishes and dirty plates and putting them away in her cart, and, pinching her fingers together in the middle of the table, she pulled off all the tablecloths with a single movement, throwing them in a large basket that she dragged along behind her. Zhang Xiangzhi asked for the check. He hadn't been speaking, just sitting there silently sweating in his gray shirt, occasionally wiping his forehead and neck with a big handkerchief. He still had his dark sunglasses on; his cheekbones glistened with sweat. We had barely communicated since the beginning of the trip (from time to time, he'd point to something in a brusque and authoritative way, my empty beer can for example, to see if I wanted another one, or the way to the bathroom, when I stood up with an indecisive look, expressively indicating the direction I should take). At times, he'd struggle to tell me something in broken English, to which, acquiescing, I would respond with a prudent smile, vague, courteous, reluctant to engage in any conversation. I had trouble understanding him, his English being rudimentary, often modeled after the monosyllabic structure of Chinese, his accent difficult to understand, he pronounced *forget* like *fuck* (*don't fuck it*, he had, for example, strongly advised me concerning the train ticket—*no, no, don't worry*, I said).

He seemed sullen, our friend Zhang Xiangzhi, slumped over in the corner of the seat, shoulder against the window, spiral toothpick sticking out of his mouth. Lost in thought, he took his cell phone out of his pocket and dialed a number. He waited for someone to pick up, looking out the window at the countryside while picking at his teeth, his face was expressionless, impassive, he spoke a few words in Chinese as though he were giving a succinct report of the situation (and, even if it wasn't likely, I couldn't keep myself from thinking that he was talking about me, so strong was the feeling that I was being kept under constant surveillance since getting to China). As the conversation picked up, he stood up with his hand on the back of my seat, and I watched him take a few steps down the aisle of the dining car, pacing back and forth through the train talking on his cell phone as though he were in his living room, waving his arms in agitation, he was getting all worked up now, his voice became sharp, angry, he began yelling into the phone, short bursts of Chinese words, brief scansions of sputtered syllables that he emitted in a submachine-gun rhythm. The most surprising part of all this is that when he hung up and sat back down with us, he didn't seem in any way bothered by the violent conversation he'd just had. He muttered a few words in Chinese to Li Qi in a bantering tone (along the lines of, "What an idiot, that We Fujing!") then swiftly slipped his tiny, Bondi-blue colored phone into the pocket of his gray shirt.

We had gone back to our bunks, and I was lying flat on my back, motionless in the heavy heat of the compartment, my attention caught by the dim glow of a blue night-light. Zhang Xiangzhi was lying on the neighboring bunk, socks and shoes removed, facing the wall with his back turned toward me (I could hear him breathing regularly, he had fallen asleep as soon we got back). Apart from the steady rumble of the train racing toward Beijing, no noise could be heard in the compartment. Li Qi was lying just above me on the middle bunk, I couldn't see her, but I could sense she wasn't sleeping, at times I heard her stirring quietly. With my eyes open in the semi-darkness, I was thinking about her, about the delicate way she looked at me, about her fruitlike name. We had already exchanged so many signs of mutual attraction since the beginning of the trip, so many suggestive looks and superficially inadvertent touches, each one a silent declaration of love, clandestine and secret. We hadn't kissed yet because circumstances hadn't lent themselves to that occasion, and it was even possible that we would never kiss. This didn't put me off—rather, I was fond of her reserve because I was fond of my own timidity. We were both aware that we liked each other, she knew it just as well as I did, and, likewise, both of us knew that the other knew it. But what was still lacking, and what would, perhaps, always be lacking, was the occasion, the opportune moment, the right time or season.

About ten minutes passed, it was really hot in the compartment, I had unbuttoned my shirt and I was sweating, lying there motionless on the bed with my arms flat by my sides. I was continuing to think about Li Qi lying above me on her bed when, in the blue half-light of the compartment, one of her feet entered my field of vision, alone and hesitant, covered with a white sock, dangling in the air above my head, then the other foot, also covered with a sock, her two feet soon followed by her whole body, twisting in slow motion, gently letting herself slide down, one foot pausing briefly on the edge of my bed before, with a tiny hop, agilely descending on the floor of the compartment. A silent and weightless silhouette, she moved around noiselessly, furtive, sandals in her hand, which she proceeded to slip on one after the other in the aisle while balancing on one leg. She turned around and gently leaned over me. She smiled at me, her finger over her lips, while our eyes met and conspired together for a fraction of a second in the complicity of the moment.

I had grabbed my bag and quietly joined Li Qi in the vestibule, and I was following her through the somnolent train, stumbling down the aisles as we passed from car to car. Having reached the dining car, we found that it was locked. There was still some light coming from the rear of the car, the kitchen was still open, a young girl was doing the dishes barefoot in a small nook in front of a metal sink filled with plates and dirty dishes. Li Qi knocked on the windowpane, tried to get someone's attention. After a moment, dragging his feet, an old cook in a white apron and creased chef's hat stained with grease came to open the door, cigarette stub hanging out of his lips, and he exchanged a few words in Chinese with Li Qi. He told her they were closed, that he couldn't sell us anything. Li Qi insisted and he went to go get us a couple of beers, which he then stashed in a crumpled plastic bag. He closed and locked the door, and we headed back, retracing our steps, the jostling of the train knocking us off balance from time to time. We crossed through silent compartments in which people slept in funerary positions on their beds amid a murmur of snores and brief coughing fits. Here and there, someone would block our path, asleep on a foldaway seat in the middle of the aisle, head lying flat on a side table. Reaching the damaged door at which I'd stopped earlier, I felt a pleasant draft of warm air touching my face, streaming in through the broken window whose absence had been so poorly repaired by a fluttering sheet of plastic held by a single strand of tape. We sat down there to drink our beers, in that intermediary space, a sort of narrow vestibule between compartments, next to the bathroom and the conductor's compartment. We sat down on the floor and began talking quietly in the somnolent train.

And we kissed there, sitting on the floor, in the roar of the train flying through the night.

Electric wires and catenaries zipped by in the sky through the filthy window of the train door. The train was hurrying through the Chinese countryside at full speed. We were going through fields and forests, passing by watercourses and grade crossings, and we were kissing seated on the floor of the train, clumsily, our arms and legs entangled. I was running my hands gently down Li Qi's bare arms, taking her hands, touching her shoulders, letting my fingers slide down her warm skin, and, when I lifted up her shirt to caress her stomach and move up along her breasts, I felt her breathing heavily in my ear and at the same time getting up, slowly rising against the wall to stand up on her feet, pulling me toward her while keeping my hand under her shirt. She whispered to me that we couldn't stay there, and, looking around anxiously, began to move away, pulling me by the arm to follow, stumbling over our beer cans which spilled out at our feet, and she lead me into the bathroom, pushed me against the sink, and pressed her lips on mine.

It was a tiny space, violently bright, with a wall mirror stained with water streaks and flecked with spots, under which was a rudimentary sink whose skinny metal faucet was operated by a foot pedal. Up higher on the wall, an opaque window, swung open, looked out into the black sky, and a moist draft of air mixed with the roaring of the train reached us with an extraordinary force. The jolts and shaking of the train were causing the poorly closed door to rattle. I had started to remove Li Qi's black strapless top, which stuck tightly to her body, and proceeded to lift it up over her head, pulling it away from her long hair to which it remained stuck for a moment due to static electricity, the shock of which ran up my fingers as if I had just grabbed onto an electric fence. I placed her top, still charged with electricity, on the edge of the sink, where it immediately bunched up into a tiny mass, and I caught a brief glimpse of our bodies reflected in the mirror, it was only a glance before turning quickly away, but the glimpsed image had left its imprint in my mind, our bodies entwined in the glaring, green-tinted light of this miniscule space, Li Qi breathing heavily in my arms, wearing nothing but black pants and her cream-colored bra, her skinny torso pressed against my body. When I tried to unhook her bra, I felt her gracefully slip away, with a supple and smooth twist of her body, breaking free from my embrace to close and latch the door. Her back against the door, motionless, she was waiting for me. I moved toward her, slid my hands behind her back and undid her bra. The straps fell, and only her jade amulet remained there around her neck, her breasts were uncovered in front of me. I reached my hand forward and began gently touching her breasts, slowly, as she arched her back against the door, moaning, pushing her pelvis against my body. Then, suddenly, we froze. Someone had tried to come into the bathroom.

We stood still, arms by our sides, we had cautiously let go of one another and we were standing there face to face without budging, Li Qi placing her finger on my lips to keep me from making any noise. Our faces motionless, extremely close together, we were looking into each other's eyes with an expression of feverish complicity. Carefully, I reached my hand forward and slid my fingers up her arm, squeezing her shoulder, noiselessly pulling her toward me again and silently holding her in my arms. The person who had tried to come in had given up, he had left, we couldn't hear any noise coming from the other side of the door apart from the steady rumbling of the train traveling through the night. But when, hardly a few seconds later, I heard a phone ring outside the bathroom, I knew right away it was the cell phone that had been given to me, ringing in my bag, and I felt my heart beat fast, I was overcome by a feeling of terror, a mix of panic, guilt, and shame. I had always maintained a difficult relationship with phones, a combination of repulsion, squeamishness, and lifelong fear, an irrepressible phobia that I no longer even tried to suppress but had finally come to terms with, handling it by using them as little as possible. I had always known more or less unconsciously that this fear was tied to death—maybe to sex and death—but never, before this night, never had I been given such an uncontestable confirmation that there is absolutely some secret alchemy connecting phones to death.

Zhang Xiangzhi was there behind the door. He hadn't succeeded in getting me to open the door of my own volition, and so had come up with this strategy to force me out. He probably hadn't been asleep when we'd left the compartment, probably was only pretending to sleep, stretched out on his bed facing the wall, listening attentively, he heard everything and knew exactly what was going on. He had gotten up as soon as we had left the compartment and followed us silently down the hall, he had watched us the whole time and was now waiting behind the bathroom door. He was lurking in the shadows in the corner of the vestibule and was eyeing the bathroom door, he was staking it out, and he was waiting for me to come out, for me to step vulnerably out into the open. I listened for any other noise in the vestibule. The phone continued to ring outside the bathroom, resonating in my head, the rings penetrating me, rattling my nerves, paralyzing my limbs while at the same time insisting that I take action, move, react, as though this were a natural reflex, requiring no thought, the unconscious obligation to answer a ringing phone. I unlocked the door and rushed into the noise, I didn't see anyone, I lunged at my backpack and quickly seized the phone while opening the connecting door and stepping into the space between the two cars, where I was greeted by a gust of hot air, a ferocious scream of air wailing through that dark space in which all other noise is suppressed by the terrifying roar of the train tearing through the night. I ran over the narrow causeway, which shook beneath my feet, over the void into the next car, I couldn't find the answer-button, I'd already been saying *allô*, *allô* into the receiver when I caught sight of the large stain of dried blood in the middle of the broken vestibule door, and, finally able to answer the phone, my eyes fixed on the loosely attached sheet of plastic fluttering wildly in the wind, I heard, as if off in the distance, Marie's faint voice.

It was Marie calling from Paris, her father had died, she'd just found out a moment ago.

What struck me the most at that moment was that she wasn't crying, not weeping, not screaming, not sobbing, her voice seemed calm, if trembling a little bit, out of breath, in a hurry to tell me, in great confusion, about the phone call she'd just received from Maurizio, the porter of her father's estate in Elba, where her father spent his summers. Maurizio had just called to inform her of her father's death, brutal, accidental, by drowning or heart failure, or both, he hadn't been that clear and now she was being even less so, she was at the Louvre right now, the Louvre Museum, collapsed on a bench, which she had struggled to reach when she had heard the news, the accident happened earlier this afternoon and it was now five o'clock in Paris, five-thirty, she didn't know, I don't know, I don't know anything, she said, it's light outside, she told me, it's horribly light out.

Marie, I figured from the rustling on the phone, had gotten up now and was trying to leave the Louvre, she was passing from room to room toward the exit, swaying, staggering, her hands trembling and the sunlight burning her eyes, she started to rush, trying to cross the two hundred meter stretch of the Grande Galerie as quickly as possible, as if trying to run away from the news she had just received, moving in search of the exit with little concern for the visitors blocking her way, elbowing her way along here, shoving there, shielding herself with her arm, leaving a wave of heads turning and muttering in disbelief and disapproval in her wake. She didn't turn back and continued to talk to me as she swerved abruptly toward where a couple of museum guards were seated to ask how to reach the exit, her voice distraught and pleading, wanting to get out of the Louvre and not listening to their directions, retracing her steps and stumbling over a tiny marble step, picking up her pace then and going through a succession of darker rooms, the Salon Carré, the Salle Duchâtel, the Salles Percier et Fontaine, leaving the glaring sunlight of the Grande Galerie behind her and taking refuge in the welcoming shade of the Rotonde d'Apollon, an enclosed and windowless space, but encountering the sun even there, like a curse, the sun seemed to be following her, an artificial one at present, counterfeit, painted, fictitious, a blazing glow on the rotunda's ceiling, while, on the shaded tympanums of nearby arches, relief sculptures added other solar motifs to this curse, sun heads dating from Louis XIV, the Sun King, crowned with halos of golden rays and adorned with flower petals of heliotropes, helianthuses, and sunflowers from which she turned her head away in desperation. Marie was staggering, Marie was losing her balance, she was stumbling down the marble stairs flooded with the light from the Winged Victory of Samothrace. Reaching the first floor, lost, one sandal barely hanging onto her foot, she strayed into a maze of vaulted rooms and began to run alongside Greek statues immobile from time immemorial, white bodies, smooth and silent, incomplete, mutilated, salvaged marble fragments impaled on metal rods that rose from cylindrical pedestals of light-colored wood, torsos and thighs removed from the rest of their bodies, hands isolated, heads hollowed, and memberless pelvises with miniscule, orphaned testicles, weaving her way around these works of art without seeing anything, as if drunk, lost among the debris from friezes and other relics of antiquity. She went down to the entresol by way of a narrow spiral staircase, went back up to the first floor. She no longer knew what she was doing, she headed back in the other direction, head lowered, no longer speaking to me, her phone brushing against her thigh as she walked, and she went to lie down on a bench, arm shielding her face from the sunlight overhead, beaming down on her, lying flat on the bench, she wasn't moving, the back of her neck was flat on the marble surface, she was looking at the vaulted ceiling, thinking about nothing at all, she was staring at a section of the painted ceiling that depicted several weightless figures in a loose conglomeration ascending in clouds, she lifted her arm slowly to bring the phone to her ear and began to describe the ceiling to me—painted with such infinite precision—in a soft and shattered voice, telling me in a whisper on the phone, across the thousands of kilometers that separated us, about the shapes and arrangements of the little clouds in the blue sky.

I was listening to Marie silently, I had closed my eyes and I could hear her voice going through my ear and into my head, where I felt it spreading and moving around in my mind. I wasn't really listening to what she was saying, startled by her news, the reality of which I had yet to fully accept, I was simply listening to her voice, the frail and sensuous texture of Marie's voice. I felt overcome by the desire to cry, and I clung to this sweet, soothing voice, I pressed the phone against my ear forcefully so that Marie's voice could penetrate into my head, into my body, pressed it so hard that it hurt, reddening my ear as I pushed the plastic phone, hot, moist, humid, against my aching temple. Eyes closed and standing still, I was listening to Marie's voice coming from thousands of kilometers away, her voice which I could hear despite the countless lands that separated us, despite the steppes and immeasurable other plains, despite the expanse of the night and its gradation of colors spread across the surface of the earth, despite the mauve light of a Siberian dusk and the first orange streaks left by a sun setting on the cities of Eastern Europe, I was listening to Marie speaking faintly in the early evening sunlight of Paris, her frail voice reaching me, sounding more or less the same as ever, in the late night of the train, literally transporting me, as thoughts, dreams, and books can do, when, releasing the mind from the body, the body remains still and the mind travels, swelling and expanding, while gradually, behind our closed eyes, images are born, and other memories, feelings, and states of being surge into view, pains and buried emotions are reawakened, as well as fears and joys and a multitude of sensations—of coldness, of heat, of being loved, of confusion—while blood pounds in our temples, our heartbeats accelerate, and we feel ourselves shaken, as if a fissure had cracked the sea of tears frozen in each of us.

I was crying. I was standing up in the train, and I was crying, silently crying, without tears or any display of emotion, my forehead sweating and my shirt unbuttoned. I stood motionless. I still had the flapping sheet of plastic in my field of vision, fluttering in the wind like a torn sail, and my mind was inundated with contradictory images of day and night, of brightness and darkness. I didn't know where I was, I could hear the train rumbling in the night, then all of a sudden I saw Li Qi appear in my field of vision, she'd quietly closed the door connecting the cars and was walking toward me in the blue half-light of the vestibule. Outside the windows trails of blazing white light streaked by joined by the glowing lights of small Chinese train stations or reflective track markers at grade crossings. Li Qi stopped when she saw my face motionless in the darkness, my unblinking eyes looking out into the night as far as they could, and she waited there for a minute in the darkness, disconcerted, next to me, not knowing what to do, timidly reaching her hand forward to place it on my shoulder. We were both standing motionless in the vestibule, and I slowly moved toward her and wrapped my arms around her, pulled her close to me without saying a word, I squeezed her tightly and lovingly against my chest, now letting my emotions come out. I had closed my eyes again and everything was mixing together in my mind, life and death, day and night, pleasure and tears, I continued to hear Marie's voice in my head and I was gently squeezing Li Qi in my arms in an embrace both of mourning and compassion that wasn't meant for her. I was rubbing her shoulders, running my fingers through her hair to comfort her. Li Qi lifted her head and sought my lips in the darkness, but I turned away instinctively, and, as our eyes met, she gave me a look as though to question what was going on, and, without saying anything—I couldn't say anything, couldn't move, couldn't explain anything to her—I continued to look at her, speechless, my expression of distress surely betraying the seriousness of what I had just learned, and she left me alone, I watched her go back into the blue darkness of the vestibule, open the connecting door, and vanish.

For a long time now I hadn't been able to hear Marie on the phone, only crackling noises, rustling, more static, then the sound of her walking, and, suddenly overtaken by dizziness, her speeding through the underground shops in the Carrousel du Louvre—her or me, I'm not sure anymore—Rue de Rivoli was deserted beyond the escalator, sidewalks broiling in the breezeless heat of a Parisian afternoon, an ambulance was parked on the other side of the road, a roadblock had been set up on Rue de Rivoli, police tape held back a throng of onlookers grouped under the arcades near a café whose terrace was in a disarray of table parasols and steel chairs, a group of people had gathered on the crosswalk and firemen were entering and exiting the scene with blankets, with oxygen, a bus was stopped at the entrance of the narrow passageway that passes beneath the arches of the Pavillon de Rohan into the Carrousel plaza, the bus had been emptied of its passengers, doors wide open, several firemen kneeling on the ground at the edge of the sidewalk were occupied with something near one of the vehicle's front tires, the bus had been elevated on one side by a system of jacks and wooden boards, the apparatuses used to remove people from wrecked vehicles were standing close by, hacksaws, thick straps, fire extinguishers and gas cans, paramedics in white uniforms were leaning over an invisible figure whose legs could just be made out—was a person stuck there under the wheels?—it was hard to see, the sun was burning her eyes, and Marie felt like she was going to faint, pass out, her chest felt weighted down, she began searching through her purse frantically, looking for her sunglasses, digging through its contents before finally dumping them all out on the sidewalk, keys, letters, passport, credit cards, all of which were piling up on top of each other on the ground now and which, squatting down on the sidewalk, she was picking back up in flustered handfuls to shove them back however she could make them fit into her purse, until at last she found her sunglasses and put them on with trembling hands and so walked off through the arcades, crossing the street and telling me that she was going to get some things from home, when our conversation was cut off in the middle of an unfinished sentence, her last words failing to reach me, forever left hovering between continents, suspended between day and night.

Marie had fallen silent, not a single sound could be heard on the phone. I hadn't budged. Forehead pressed against the window, my body numb, the only thing in my mind was a string of meaningless words, "*Henri de Montalte has died*," and I continued to stare at the dark night through the window. I was hot, I was sweating, I felt my forehead dripping, sweat was streaming down my temples and I didn't care to wipe it off. I finally decided to move, I went back to where I'd been sitting with Li Qi a little bit earlier. There wasn't anyone in the abandoned vestibule, only beer cans tipped over on the ground, empty, and a little puddle of yellow beer on the floor, softly bubbling, a trace left from our previous encounter. I didn't know where I was going, I was hot, I tried to open a window in the hallway but I couldn't find any handle on the thing and I had no patience, I gave up and continued on my way. I finally found a window already cracked in the middle of another hallway and I stopped there to try to open it even more, pushing down hard with both hands on the thin pane of glass. With force, slowly, I was able to push the window down, millimeter by millimeter, as though it were necessary to pry the walls of the train open to reach the night air. As soon as I was able to open the window completely—the window was wide open now, gaping in the middle of the hall, like the side door of a freight car, directly overhanging the tracks—braving the overwhelming feeling of terror and the screaming hot air that surged in around me, I stuck my head through the window and leaned out over the abyss. Scorching hot air lashed against my face, I could make out tall black grass on the hillsides and see dust and dirt swirling up along the trackside due to the force of the train's passing. Leaning out the window, I could feel the horizon and the curvature of the earth gliding and spinning underneath me, I could see power lines obliquely rising and falling in the sky, fugitive electric poles appearing for a second before vanishing from sight, quickly swallowed by the speed of the train leaving them behind, frozen in place. With the wind pressing my shirt against my chest and stinging my eyes, sand and dust flying directly into my face, as well as bits of clay and miniscule pieces of gravel, my view began to cloud over, and, in an aqueous fog, trembling and dimly illuminated, my mist-filled eyes formed blinding tears in the black night.

II

The train arrived in Beijing a little before 9 A.M. I don't remember anything, I followed Zhang Xiangzhi and Li Qi through the train station, my bag over my shoulder, we didn't say a word, we got caught in the middle of a packed crowd of travelers carrying bags and bundles. The exits of the central train station had been closed for repair and renovation, we had to follow a detour made of plywood boards in order to leave the station. This was my first contact with the city (it was the first time I visited Beijing), a little zigzagging arrangement of uneven boards placed directly on the ground, which we followed in a straight line over an ochre-colored dirt path. Slowly, above our heads, the skinny metal arms of giant cranes twisted in the white sky while hot air, heavy, acrid, oppressive, filled with sand and dust, swirled in front of our eyes amid the noise of hammers and pneumatic drills, whose pounding shook the earth in the sweltering heat of that morning.

I paused for a moment outside the train station, awed by the sun and the noise, by the city, the heat, dust, and traffic. Zhang Xiangzhi hailed a cab and we got in while he gave the driver the address to our hotel. I didn't know where we were going, I didn't know what was going to happen. I sat in the backseat of the cab, Zhang Xiangzhi had gotten in front and was directing the driver, reprimanding him, giving him a piece of his mind (no matter what the circumstances, his Chinese always sounded violent). Li Qi, by my side, remained quiet, casting furtive glances at me from time to time, kind and well-meaning, she didn't insist on making sense of my coldness toward her, my distance, seemingly unconcerned by the invisible barrier that I had put up between us since Marie's phone call on the train. Our kisses the previous night seemed so strange and faraway to me now, the only memory I had was of a dream-like pleasure, distant and hazy. I hadn't told her anything about the death of Marie's father, I hadn't said anything to anyone, and our relationship was now even more enigmatic than it had been at the beginning of the trip. Forehead sweating, eyes unblinking, I watched the streets file by out the window, we passed cars and motorcycles, a flood of beat-up, two-wheeled carts lugging any and everything through traffic, cabbage, ears of corn, dried chili peppers, a heap of old computers, live chickens stacked in cages zooming through the streets cackling and leaving bits of straw swirling in the air behind them.

Reaching the hotel, Zhang Xiangzhi asked to see the manager and followed him into a private office. We waited for him in the lobby, a large, impersonal space with glass walls and an empty bar where an employee was vacuuming under some empty tables. The hotel seemed to be under construction, with beams, girders, and scaffolding rails piled here and there. A small store was open but had nothing for sale, the display tables were empty, the shelves covered in plastic. Further along, at a recess in the wall, a smoked-glass door opened into a closed-down "business center," where large cylindrical rolls of wallpaper had been left leaning against the walls. I glanced over a few tourist flyers posted at the entranceway that advertised day trips to the Great Wall at Badaling or Mutianyu, with low-quality illustrations emphasizing less the beauty of the sites than the comforts of an air-conditioned Pullman train. When Zhang Xiangzhi returned to the lobby, he told us that he'd been able to negotiate a good price for the rooms with the manager (I didn't say anything, I didn't react in any way, I was going with the flow).

The hotel's only elevator was temporarily out of service, it was stopped in the lobby with its doors propped open, a technician in shorts was kneeling on the ground, a black welder's mask covering his face, in the middle of doing some repair work in a small explosive spray of blue and white sparks. Zhang Xiangzhi walked passed the broken elevator and opened the heavy fire door to the service stairs, using the flame of his lighter to lead us up the dark stairwell. On the third floor we went out into a hallway filled with paint supplies, tin cans, metal bins, buckets, and jerricans. The floor, over a stretch of about ten meters, was protected by a transparent plastic cover, and we had to make our way down this soft, undulant path to reach our rooms, our feet sinking in clumps of polyethylene, making the plastic crackle at each step. We walked down this long deserted hall, passing by a succession of doorless rooms (these must have been removed, or perhaps had never existed), and, glancing in as we passed, we'd notice, framed in the doorways, the silhouettes of young painters, shirtless, pirate turbans on their heads, painting with rollers and listening to the radio at full volume in empty spaces in which particles of plaster danced in the liquid light of an oblique sunbeam. Other rooms, further along, were in a similar unfinished state, beautiful hardwood floors in the process of being sanded, bare walls covered with only a single coating of paint, windows flung wide-open offering views of the street, no beds, no furniture, sometimes a new white enamel sink lying in wait on the floor in the middle of a room. I was beginning to wonder if the hotel, rather than being renovated, was simply being built, just now, for the first time, with construction workers perched on scaffolding above us, working in the open air outside to put the finishing touches on the roof (in which case it made sense that Zhang Xiangzhi could have negotiated a good price with the manager). We entered a hall that had seemingly just been remodeled, with new carpet and pale yellow wallpaper, and Zhang Xiangzhi stopped at a door, opened it and invited me in, letting me know that it was my room. At this point I was almost on the verge of saying something—that I had to go back to Europe—but I didn't speak, I stood there at my doorstep and watched the two of them continue down the hall, Li Qi turned back to risk a glance at me over her shoulder, they had only taken a few steps more before stopping at a door on the other side of the hall. Zhang Xiangzhi slid a magnetic key card into the lock and I saw them both enter the same room—and it wasn't until then that it occurred to me, for the first time, that they might once have been lovers, or perhaps still were.

In my room I immediately made a few phone calls to arrange my return flight. At first I could only get through to an operator who kept saying *ouais* to me in a glum voice (actually, she was saying *wei*, "hello" in Chinese, which sounds very much like *ouais*, which is "yeah" in French, and tends to get spoken with the same level of casualness and fatigue). Finally, after several unsuccessful attempts to reach the travel agency where

I had purchased my ticket, I got hold of an Air France branch in Beijing and was able, for an extra charge, to change my ticket to arrive in Paris the following day (I was now registered on AF Flight #129, departing tomorrow morning). I stretched out on the bed, exhausted, my mind clear, and I fell asleep almost immediately (I couldn't tell you how many times I've slept like this). When I woke up the sun was filling the room, it was humid, I was sweating, I was completely dressed, my shirt was sticking to me, I hadn't showered since the previous night, I hadn't taken off my shoes. I groped my way to the bathroom and I examined my face in the mirror, expressionless, rings under my swollen eyes, a vacant look, inscrutable, still sleepy, eyes a worn gray color with a faint glint of silver, veiled by the almost milky white of the cornea, which was marked by small, burst blood vessels. A murmur of inarticulate street noise, sounds of engines and car horns, reached the room, softened by the double-paned glass of the hotel windows. I walked over to the window, the panes were dirty, smudged with dirt and filth, with the residue of urban pollution stuck like a coating to the glass. I looked at the street below, at the morning traffic of Beijing, buses caught in traffic jams, passersby, strange, distant, who seemed to be moving more through the thick fog of my imagination than in the actual streets of Beijing. Since the previous night, since Marie's phone call in the train, I was perceiving the world as if in a state of perpetual jet lag, causing a slight distortion in the fabric of reality, a shift, a misalignment, giving rise to a miniscule yet fundamental incompatibility between the familiar world around me and the removed way, distant and hazy, in which I perceived it.

After showering (I had put on a clean shirt and was feeling a little better), I left the room and knocked on the door across the hall. After a short wait, Zhang Xiangzhi opened it a crack, his face distrustful, phone held to his ear. He invited me in without saying a word, greeting me with a nod and motioning for me to sit down on the bed. The room was almost identical to mine, same twin beds, same wallpaper, same accessories and small bedside lamps, but it had already been thrown into a remarkable disorder, clothes strewn everywhere, on the backs of chairs, on the TV, a pair of pants on the ground, a pile of clean t-shirts stacked on the desk next to a dirty tea tray, with cups in disarray and used tea bags, sagging, bathing in small ponds of brown tea. Running water could be heard behind the bathroom door (Li Qi must have been taking a shower, I recognized her clothes scattered next to her open suitcase). I'd hardly sat down on the bed when the bathroom door opened and Li Qi appeared in a nimbus of steam, a small bath towel wrapped around her body and another towel, larger, thick and soft, tied around her hair. She smiled and approached me, trailing the steamy fragrances of shampoo and bath gel, readjusting the little towel around her waist in order to better hide her nudity (but each time she pulled the bottom part of the towel down, she would reveal the contours of her breasts a little bit more). She walked around a chair on which some socks were drying, and went to grab a tiny pair of panties from her suitcase, no more than a few grams of light-colored fabric that she bunched up in the palm of her hand before darting back to the bathroom.

Li Qi continued to get ready, she crossed the room several times, lost in thought, looking for a brush in her suitcase or drying her hair in front of the window. Zhang Xiangzhi suggested we go get something to eat at a small restaurant he knew close to the hotel, and we were on the verge of leaving the room when I witnessed a troubling scene in the mirror in front of me. Li Qi was practically ready, hair done and make-up applied, and she was putting some papers into her handbag, when I saw Zhang Xiangzhi approach her silently, by the bed, stepping over the trail of moist towels crumpled up on the carpet, and hand her the large manila envelope that contained the twenty-five thousand dollars in cash that I had given him on Marie's behalf when I first arrived in Shanghai. He had intentionally done this behind my back, after having made sure that

I wasn't looking or paying attention, and I felt a strange uneasiness. Of course, it could have been another envelope—though I doubted it, because I had seen it clearly, same manila paper color, same size, same small bulge from the bundles of cash—and of course there was no reason to assume that it still contained the twenty-five thousand dollars. Naturally, Zhang Xiangzhi could have taken the money out and put other documents in for Li Qi instead. Otherwise, why give the money to Li Qi? What was it for?

The restaurant Zhang Xiangzhi led us to, a few blocks from the hotel, in the middle of a busy boulevard packed with people, had nothing especially Chinese about it (it simply was what it was, and made no effort to make its character any more apparent). The walls were white, without decoration or adornment, without lacquerware with pictures of palanquins, and there were a few round tables in a large, two-level dining area. A young man in black pants and a white shirt with his sleeves rolled up greeted Zhang Xiangzhi at the door, and led us to a large round table on the mezzanine and invited us to sit down. I sat down next to Li Qi, and, looking around listlessly, my eyes settled on a large empty aquarium that had just been drained. The fish, temporarily placed in plastic buckets that were lined up in a row on a neighboring table, were swimming in circles in these yellow containers, creating small ripples and making faint lapping noises as they splashed. Their trajectories could be followed through the transparent, cream-colored sides of the buckets. The aquarium, empty, dried out, with its water tubes rolled up in its interior, was set on a sort of cabinet whose doors were open, revealing a pressurized canister and a maze of rusted pipes between the bends of which wriggled the acrobatically twisted body of a squatting man, head swallowed by his shoulders, arms deep in the pipes, struggling to fix or undo something with a screwdriver. This man, under the aquarium, whom I continued to watch distractedly while Zhang Xiangzhi ordered from the menu, unscrewed a few more bolts above his head and, detaching the last safety lock, was at last able to lift the hatch at the top of the cabinet up with both hands, cautiously, and his head now popped into the aquarium with a look of irritation and concern (he even nodded at me in a sort of greeting when our eyes met).

I wasn't eating much, I wasn't hungry. I lingered over my food, carelessly picking at minuscule pieces of whitish fish skin with my chopsticks, which I ate with tiny clusters of rice that I had to struggle to swallow. I watched Li Qi eating hungrily across from me and speaking Chinese with Zhang Xiangzhi, relaxed, smiling, composed, her gestures serene, effortlessly wielding her chopsticks. Completely absorbed in their own conversation, they had stopped bothering to translate for me, Li Qi simply let me know that she'd be busy the whole day and that Zhang Xiangzhi would show me around Beijing. From time to time, continuing to talk and serving themselves more tea, placing the lid upside down on the teapot when it was empty in order to ask for more hot water, they'd rotate the large circular tray on the table slightly to bring a specific dish within reach of their chopsticks and to pick at a piece of fish here, a bit of spiced pork there, which they'd hardly let touch the inside of their bowls before bringing them up to their mouths. I watched the tray rotate in front of me, and, since my perception of the table shifted each time the tray moved—whereas the dishes remained stable on their bases, and their positions relative to the table remained unchanging—it seemed to me that a change in perspective was also beginning to alter the relationship between the three of us, relative to its configuration the previous night, and that the innumerable mysterious questions that had till now remained unanswered—specifically, why Zhang Xiangzhi had come with us to Beijing—were now being revealed in a new light, and even finding themselves logical explanations of the utmost simplicity, as I began to get a clearer understanding—or believed I was getting a clearer understanding, since many things still remained obscure—of the situation. I realized then that if Zhang Xiangzhi had come along with us to Beijing, it wasn't for some hypothetical reason tainted with malevolent or Machiavellian intent, but simply because Li Qi must have asked him to come keep me company and show me the city while she was busy (so that what I had seen as an accidental slip on Li Qi's part, maybe even carelessness, was, on the contrary, a thoughtful gesture). Similarly, Zhang Xiangzhi's near-constant presence at my side since we'd left Shanghai, which I had at first received with distrust, even jealously, with a sort of petty small-mindedness that had caused me to see him as nothing more than an inopportune obstacle who existed to frustrate my plans, was also to be read as kind and considerate behavior on his part. And I realized then, while watching them eat across from me, that each time either one of them rotated the tray to bring a dish within reach of their chopsticks, a new shape was being configured in space, which in truth didn't indicate any sort of change in our situation, but was, rather, a case of my being presented with a different facet of the same and only reality. And, reaching my arm out to join in, I took the edge of the tray and slowly rotated it in the middle of the table, wondering what new configuration of reality would then be offered to us—since perhaps there were still surprises in store for me.

The tray had come to a stop, and I was looking at the dishes arranged on the table in front of me, minced pork with chili peppers, kidneys, skinned fish of which nothing remained now except the bones, duck tongues marinating in the remains of a brown sauce, full and complete tongues that must have been removed in their entireties from the pit of the throat, taken out from the larynx and elongated and stretched to their extremity, and I suddenly gagged when, staring at one of those little dead tongues, the image of Li Qi's tongue flashed through my mind—and this terrifying image, which I tried to forget as soon as it had popped into my head, interfered with and in a way poisoned the memory I'd kept of the real sensation, tender, sweet, of Li Qi's tongue in my mouth that night on the train, and, in place of this delightful memory there rose a feeling of disgust, of horror, of physical revulsion, the concrete, almost gustative sensation of having had one of these stretched, brownish-pink duck tongues, spotted with white and rough taste buds, in my mouth that night—soft and slithering voluptuously around my own tongue.

In the afternoon, as planned, Zhang Xiangzhi showed me around Beijing. He'd arranged an itinerary of visits consisting of two temples chosen less for their historic or religious merit, I think, than for their convenient geographic location in the northeast corner of the city and their remarkable proximity to the Yonghegong subway stop, close to which, toward seven o'clock, I later found out, he had a meeting. Throughout the whole sweltering afternoon he led me through picturesque streets whose primary importance lay in the fact that they were close to the Yonghegong subway stop, the whole tour restricted to an extremely small perimeter of four streets, bordered in the south by Dongzhimennei Dajie and in the north by Andingmendong Dajie (reaching up further along to the Andingmen subway stop, our northernmost reference point, before turning around and heading back through the same shaded streets). We walked up and down the streets of this little square kilometer of the city, which didn't lack charm, even importance. Glum, hands in pockets, he dragged his feet alongside of me through streets lined with hundred-year-old cypresses, a grumpy, morose expression on his face at all times. For the most part he remained silent, offering very little commentary, but at times, grudgingly carrying out his duties as a taciturn cicerone, he'd point out an old wooden archway covered in flaking paint that I was meant to appreciate as we passed by, muttering in an uninspired English that the street we were on was one of the last in Beijing to still have four archways (I nodded my head, and we paused there for further touristy remarks). In spite of his attitude of overwhelming fatigue, further exacerbated by the afternoon heat, he demonstrated a continual kindness toward me, and went to great lengths to ensure my comfort and enjoyment in countless unobtrusive ways. Since the previous night, he had taken care of all our hotel and restaurant expenses, and had made a concerted effort to tend to my most minor concerns: before serving me, he'd rinse all my glasses and bowls with hot tea; I couldn't even gesture toward putting my backpack down on the floor before he'd jump up and grab it delicately, as if it were an object too precious to touch the filthy Chinese ground, placing it on the soft velvet of a seat next to us; he protected me from peddlers wanting to ask me questions or sell me tourist pamphlets, and he chased off approaching beggars too (he even shooed mosquitoes away from my face with slow swipes of his hand). At times, walking ahead of me on the deserted sidewalks, smoldering with heat, he'd lead me into one of the innumerable souvenir shops on Yonghegong Dajie, filled with Buddhist religious items, where one could find all sorts of candles as well as a variety of incense—pink, purple, violet, or amaranth, in cones, sticks, or spirals. He encouraged me to take my time in the aisles, preferring to wait for me at the register, where, leaning on the counter, handkerchief in hand, he chatted with the cashier, his face planted in front of a fan whose benevolent blades stirred the heavy air of the store. I had the feeling that his only reason for accompanying me on this tourist outing was to keep me happy; that, for his part, he wasn't the least bit interested in the places we were visiting. His disinterest, it seemed, could only be rivaled by my own indifference.

Leaving the store (I didn't buy anything, but he didn't even seem to notice), we headed back through those long and shaded streets, already becoming familiar to me. I followed him down the dusty, sun-beaten sidewalk, looking at whatever my eyes happened to fall upon: a building front, a gray, granular wall where indecipherable slogans effaced by time remained partially legible. The building's gate was open, a school or post office, and an old man in a twill vest sat in the shade under a small barred window, a straw hat on his head. We walked alongside thick stone walls, behind which the glazed tiles of a peaceful sanctuary could be seen, tucked away and hidden, as though in retreat from the world. Zhang Xiangzhi had gone up to the ticket counter to buy passes, and we walked through a cluster of silent courtyards and deserted gardens, all with a very welcoming atmosphere. I had gone to sit on the curved ledge of a stone pond, which at one time must have contained water and floating lotuses, but which, at the moment, was empty, the stone bare and gray, dried out, as if all its moisture had been sucked away by the burning sun. We were alone in this abandoned courtyard, separated from one another by about twenty meters. There wasn't a single shaded corner nor the slightest breeze, just the flailing sun, heavy and vertical, invisible in the pervasive white light of the sky. Stone turtles remained impassive in the courtyard, mineral creatures with reptilian heads glistening in the blaze of the sun. Time seemed to have stopped, no longer moving, held in place, congealed in the near-visible emanations of heat.

This heat was enveloping my body and numbing my mind, drops of sweat ran down my face and neck. I opened my backpack in search of a handkerchief and I came across the little gift Li Qi had given me the previous night at the train station, and which I still hadn't opened. I unwrapped it seated there on the ledge of the pond, removed the many layers of its packaging and was surprised to find a small bottle of perfume, square-shaped, containing an aquamarine liquid, luminescent and transparent, in thick glass with three letters that looked like apocryphal roman numerals: BLV. I examined the bottle more closely and read: *Eau de parfum Vaporisateur Natural Spray 0.86 fl. oz.* It was extremely odd, and even a bit cruel, to find this perfume now, but I couldn't keep myself from being moved by the thought that, the previous night, in Shanghai, knowing she'd see me the following day, Li Qi had gone into a store with the intention of buying me a gift (and then I felt the peculiar pleasure that comes from knowing you exist in someone else's mind, that you move around there and lead an independent, inconspicuous existence).

I tilted the bottle to squirt a little eau de toilette on my wrist and then brought it up to my nose. With a twinge of sorrow, I recognized Li Qi's fragrance, the fragrance of her skin and neck—and I was struck by a very painful pleasure. I looked over at Zhang Xiangzhi, but he hadn't noticed anything, he was on the phone on the other side of the courtyard, leaning against a balustrade made of white stone. I didn't move, but I instinctively hid the bottle in the palm of my hand. I looked around, there was nobody near me. Further off, workers were busy with shovels in a space enclosed by stakes and ropes in front of a pagoda that was undergoing restoration and was covered with scaffolding. I continued to look around me, with the bottle completely hidden in the palm of my hand. I pretended to be observing the layout of the gardens and the architecture of the temple, and, almost without moving, still seated on the ledge of the pond, I slid my arm behind my back and discretely placed the bottle at the bottom of the empty pond, hiding it under a stone and abandoning it there. I stood up immediately and moved off toward the far end of the courtyard, adjusting my bag on my shoulder as if nothing had happened. I went around the courtyard and headed toward a glass pavilion, tucked away from everything else, where I wandered for a little while around black-marbled, headstone-like stelae inscribed with the graceful curves of imperial calligraphy before being chased out of the structure by the suffocating heat pervading it. When I stepped back out into the courtyard, it was empty, Zhang Xiangzhi had disappeared, no one was over by the balustrade where he'd been on the phone a few minutes earlier. I headed toward the exit, stopping for a moment in a tiny gift shop where dusty postcards were on sale. When I walked out, I looked around for Zhang Xiangzhi, and I spotted him in the distance walking in my direction down a flagstone path lined with cypress trees. He joined me under the archway, and it wasn't until right then—I noticed the spark of blue liquid glistening in the sun—that I saw he had the perfume bottle in his hand. *Don't fuck that*, he said, handing it to me with a smile of mysterious satisfaction.

Back outside, he picked up his pace (all of a sudden he seemed in a rush), we crossed a very busy street, got caught for a moment in the middle of traffic, suddenly stopped, our momentum arrested, then we passed through a few commercial streets where we struggled to work our way through the crowds, then escaped into a narrow back alley no wider than the width of my shoulders. I followed him between high gray walls with a skinny gutter running along them and then we entered a neighborhood of hutongs and winding alleyways, low-slung houses and interior courtyards and neglected patios, where a few weeds slithered their way out into the air through the interstices between the debris and rubble. We came into a deserted courtyard, no shade, an old cloth patio chair alone in the sun and car doors stacked against a wall, a few bumpers, a pile of truck tires. There was a workshop in the back of the courtyard, Zhang Xiangzhi went over and stuck his head in through the door and I heard him call out for someone several times. After a short wait, the owner appeared, slowly, in an orange mechanic's uniform unzipped down to his bellybutton, his face smeared with grease, balding, brow wrinkled, a cigarette stub hanging out of his lips, distrustful, unwelcoming. He looked me up and down without saying a word when Zhang Xiangzhi introduced me, and had us go into the workshop. At the back of the shop, in humid shadows reeking of hot oil, two mechanics wearing sandals were playing foosball, standing in a layer of metal filings, while a few men in floral-printed Bermudas worked underneath an elevated car (a new Western car, a huge black BMW with tinted windows, which clashed a bit with the décor). The shop owner walked over to a work bench covered with tools and unscrewed the lid of a thermos to serve us both a complimentary glass of tea, very light, almost colorless (I swished it around in my small cup and took a sip, realizing that it was water, just plain old hot water). He continued to talk to Zhang Xiangzhi in Chinese, who participated in the conversation by nodding his head, looking down from time to time at the bottom of his cup. The shop owner called over one of his apprentices, a little fifteen- or sixteen-year-old guy, who led us to an annex of the shop, two or three streets away, unlocking an imposing brass padlock and taking it off an old wooden door, chipped and rotting, inviting us into a small shop with a vaulted ceiling, extremely dark and overheated, stuffy, with no skylight, containing an enormous collection of motorcycles. Zhang Xiangzhi walked between the bikes, checking them out, every type imaginable was there, old models, Chinese, Russian, old English varieties, new bikes, sparkling Japanese models, used bikes with every number of cylinder, wrecked bikes, bikes without wheels, chassis without parts (and even an old Singer sewing machine, black, pedal-driven, which probably wouldn't even reach twenty kilometers per hour going downhill). From time to time, he fiddled with one, adjusting the handlebars, feeling the thin leather of a seat, crouching down to look more closely at an engine, scratching the finish with his fingernail. He ended up choosing an old Norton with a round headlight and a Chinese license plate attached to its curved fender. The bike (its tank smoothly convex, a burgundy color with hints of mahogany) looked like it had been fixed up recently, a few parts had been changed, a new swingarm had been added, as well as a new seat made of black leatherette, extended, curved. We left the shop, Zhang Xiangzhi pushing the bike through the street.

He left the motorcycle with the apprentice back in the courtyard and went to find the shop owner, who took us into his office in the shop, a shabby glass room with broken windows and a couple of rolling chairs dotted with flyspecks, the floor greasy, slippery, a metal table piled sloppily with old magazines, pliers, screwdrivers, and rags, all of which he swept to the floor with the back of his arm in order to clear a space for an extra-thin titanium-gray laptop. While Zhang Xiangzhi, sitting on a stool, went over a contract, the shop owner, with a tense and focused look, leaning over the computer glowing in the half-light, tapped its touchpad to check a box on the screen, thereby rousing his printer, like a cat startled from its nap, invisible till now in the prevailing torpor, resting on the more-or-less unlit floor between a pile of rusted tools and an old red and black box of Champion spark plugs, now beginning to discharge, stroke by stroke, as it were, a full page of Chinese characters. Careful not to touch the printed page with his fingers, blackened by grease, the shop owner used a screwdriver to remove the sheet, carefully balancing it and presenting it thus to Zhang Xiangzhi, who grabbed it listlessly and glanced over it before folding it in four and putting it in his pocket. Was it a document concerning the bike, a renter's agreement, proof of purchase, receipt, insurance form? I had no idea. In any case, it appeared that the bike had been entrusted to Zhang Xiangzhi. Before leaving, the shop owner gave him an old helmet, white, small, dirty, thick, with a tiny visor, and we left the shop to join the apprentice, who was polishing the bike's gas tank with chamois leather at the courtyard's entrance. Zhang Xiangzhi exchanged a few words with him, sat on the bike, and started it. Both hands on the grips of the handlebars, he began to rev up the engine in a cloud of black, foul-smelling exhaust. He handed me the helmet and told me to get on behind him. I'd barely sat down when he turned around and took the helmet from my hands, explaining that it would be better for him to wear it just in case we were stopped by the police (sure, and in case of an accident too). He adjusted it on his head, tying the chinstrap with care.

We were on our way, moving slowly, kicking up dust in the street, skirting the rubble and potholes and the large stones and small heaps of bricks that blocked the road. I hung on behind him, and I could feel the incessant wobbling of the bike caused by the very limited speed we were forced to travel at as we passed pedestrians, and by our constant swerving, provoked by a sometimes sudden jerk of the handlebars in order to dodge the unforeseeable dash of a barefooted kid running out in front of us, or some elderly person inching across the street, whom we'd always just barely miss. Here and there cackling chickens evaded our tires, running away in a whirl of feathers and taking refuge under the legs of mah-jongg players seated around a low table at the entrance of a bird shop, where cages of all sizes, chirping and cooing, were clustered around the door and stacked against the windows. The pits and rocks in the street continued to redirect our course as we rode on, following long unpaved roads lined with tiny food stands, going through narrow alleys thronged with street vendors, many of whom blocked our way with rickety handcarts wobbling under heavy masses of fruit and vegetables, before finally emerging onto a large avenue, where we momentarily stopped the bike and put our feet down—contemplating the dense flow of Beijing traffic spilling tumultuously in every direction, as if, after having sailed through a number of small canals, we had suddenly reached the great sea—before throwing ourselves into the current with a new burst of speed, letting ourselves be pulled along by the rush of buses and taxis, picking up speed among the steady flow of cars heading south on Beijing's elevated freeways.

We were weaving our way between vehicles to pass through car-filled roundabouts, continuing to accelerate, slicing forward at breakneck speeds, faces against the wind, passing rows of sand- and plaster-colored apartment blocks, single concrete masses with cheap white tiling, and administrative centers or government offices with soldiers on guard out front, when I suddenly saw the monumental portrait of Mao appear above the entrance of the Forbidden City to my left, and, fleetingly, in accordance with the speed of the motorcycle, never faltering, the famous rose-colored walls of the Imperial Palace—leading Zhang Xiangzhi, in front of me, to let go of the handlebars briefly, in order to point at the building, screaming "*Gugong, Gugong*!" to me, all while giving a thumbs-up in the wind, presumably to express how much he admired the palace (and with this same gesture implicitly advising me, in a way, to visit it), and so, clinging onto him, with my view blocked by an old green and yellow bus that was then passing us, I turned around to get one last look at the string of pagoda tops on the Forbidden City, already vanishing in the distance (so this, then, was my visit: I'd hardly had time to recognize the City before we'd already left it behind).

The thin blanket of pink-colored fog that covered the city was giving way to black clouds of urban pollution on the horizon. Sitting on the back of the bike, I could smell an acrid urban odor in the hot wind that beat against my face. It was the air of the earlier daytime, still heavy with all the heat accumulated by the walls and the asphalt, by the sidewalks and the stone of the buildings, as if the urban scenery had preserved the thermal memory of the sweltering day, and now its sediment of black smoke, exhaust, and dust had become fossilized in the thinning air. I'm not sure exactly when I realized—or sensed, rather, since my geographic understanding of Beijing was rudimentary at best—that we weren't headed back to the hotel, that it was actually impossible to reach the hotel from where we were. We were on a service road alongside the freeway, riding in a darkening, increasingly nocturnal light, racing toward a bloodstained horizon, with the pink color of the sky turning red and the gray turning black, and we passed the night's first headlights in the semidarkness of a freeway where vehicles began to blur and lose definition in the twilit hours, we were passing through a moment in time that was not yet night but still held the last dying flames of day. Zhang Xiangzhi hadn't said a word to me, hadn't explained anything to me, and once again I let myself go with the flow, not asking any questions. I'm not sure if we had left Beijing, our surroundings resembled one of those indistinct zones found around airports or else one of those industrial areas with their vast expanses of warehouses on the outskirts of cities, countless lights shone in the vague crepuscular light, the white headlights of cars stuck in traffic jams or red lights of descending planes approaching invisible runways. We had exited the service road, and we turned onto a busy city street, with clusters of buildings and high-rises, large gated courtyards, and glass-box guardhouses in which uniformed security men were keeping watch. Zhang Xiangzhi slowed down and turned into an immense multi-story parking complex where bright signs flashed like hazard lights in the night, some in Chinese characters, white and green, others in English, pink, blue, red, directing our attention to the karaoke bars and nightclubs, bowling alley, and restaurants accessible via the various floors of the lot. An oversized sign stood out from the bunch, reigning supreme atop the roof of the structure and seemingly baptizing the entire complex with its fairytale name, LAS VEGAS, composed of pink neon letters and thronged by two fluorescent-blue lightning bolts, silently striking the night.

Zhang Xiangzhi parked the motorcycle in the lot. A group of teenagers had congregated by the bowling alley's underground entrance, which was lit up with an arc of yellow bulbs, auburn-haired girls in leather miniskirts, all done up, guys in tight fitting white t-shirts and ultra-thin suede jackets, thumbs in pockets, watching us get off the bike, staring at us conspicuously as we passed by. Zhang Xiangzhi told me we were going to meet up with Li Qi before dinner. We went into the stairwell and started walking down the stairs. There were small groups of young people clustered almost everywhere in the stairwell, chatting pressed against the wall or massed in semi-circles on the stairs themselves. The bowling alley was located on the second sublevel, forty or so lanes aligned in a hall with low ceilings, the steady rumble of tumbling pins mixing with the uproar of bowlers shouting and cheering and the blaring disco music supplemented by the spinning and flashing disco balls, reflectors, and rotating multicolor spotlights. Video screens suspended above the lanes posted the perpetually fluctuating scores of ongoing matches. Zhang Xiangzhi walked over to the bar and sat down on a stool, looking out at the lanes. His face was swept by reflections of green and red lights that danced across his forehead in fleeting waves. *Play bowling?* he asked me after a pause. I nodded, thoughtfully. *Play?* he asked. *Yes*, I said. I wasn't sure I understood what he wanted, but it didn't matter, I said yes—I had played before, I wouldn't mind playing now.

I sat there alone while Zhang Xiangzhi went to reserve a lane. There was a diverse crowd in the bowling alley, young for the most part, smoking and striking poses in front of giant screens showing looped clips of Asian bowling matches intercut with music videos. A group of young people would congregate at the bar as their friends ordered drinks and then head back to the lanes with a loose bouquet of paper cups that they'd protect with steady hands. Here and there, to the sides of the lanes, small groups of girls would react to any whack of pins set off by a friend's ball with loud, celebratory shouts, just as they'd let out cries of despair, mixed with a little conflicted joy, whenever a friend's feeble throw, whose course they followed closely with strident laughs of terror and delight, fell into the gutter (leaving one young girl crouching alone in the lane, both hands over her mouth). A few lanes at the far end of the hall were reserved for more experienced bowlers, young men and women with their own equipment and accessories behind them in open bowling bags: their own shoes and balls, black pants and prune-colored bowling shirts with stitched logos, openwork gloves made of beige leather (that keep one's fingers exposed and maneuverable, like fingerless mittens) or else wrist supports, small bracelets of thick black leather to help one's arm maintain the proper form when releasing a ball. Before bowling, they'd polish their ball meticulously with a dry rag, then position themselves in their lanes and concentrate a moment before finally beginning their surge forward, leaning extremely close to the ground while giving a lot of sidespin to their ball, which would begin by veering off to the left before curving back to the center of the lane abruptly to knock down every last pin, sounding the indisputable crash of a strike.

After a few minutes, Zhang Xiangzhi came back over and told me that a lane was being freed for us, so we went to exchange our shoes at a counter behind which an old poster announced, in English, as if proclaiming an absurd (or metaphysical) injunction: *BORN TO BOWL*. I put my shoes on the counter and was given an old pair of cream-leather bowling shoes in exchange, smooth and creased, the heel black and the Velcro straps crimson, the soles slick as ice. Whereas Zhang Xiangzhi selected the bowling ball he was going to play with rather carefully, inspecting every model available on the different racks before picking one of the more extravagant examples, made of a black and green composite material that looked like overchewed gum, I simply tested the weight of two or three balls from the ball-return rack in our lane, pensively, before choosing one that seemed to work for me. But—before my first turn, I was suddenly overcome by a feeling of languor and despondency. I stood looking at our lane, ball poised at chin level, and I concentrated on the pins in front me, but I was unable to move forward, incapable of connecting the movement I intended my arm to make with my intended targets, incapable of coordinating my hand and my eye, so I lingered there indecisively, paralyzed, my legs without strength, trembling beneath me, getting weaker as I remained motionless in front of the lane, the ball becoming heavier and heavier in my hand, I didn't see any way of getting out of this, and I probably would have stayed stuck like that, or else would finally have given up, would have turned around and gone to sit back down without ever taking my turn, if I hadn't heard Zhang Xiangzhi behind me, saying, with a touch of annoyance, then of frustration, as if giving a strict order, finally almost screaming, *Play!*

I had completely ruined my first turn (and didn't do much better with the following ones). Zhang Xiangzhi, silent and grumpy, steadily accumulated points, his style smooth and effective, unembellished, effortless, his delivery straight and powerful, the result consistently impressive. There wasn't the slightest trace of deliberation in his approach, just pure force and instinct. We played in silence, we hadn't exchanged a single word since the beginning of the match. I'd take my turn and sit back down, wait, watch him take his turn. I had no other thoughts in my head apart from those concerning our match, concentrating on my next turn, my next ball hitting the pins. I had been transported to another universe since we'd begun playing, an abstract space, interior, conceptual, with softened edges, marked by an absence of suffering. Little by little the chaos of the bowling alley fell silent around me, the noise of the blaring music and the futile shouting of other bowlers failed to reach me in my new state of mind. I was alone before the lane, my ball in hand, my eyes focused on my sole objective, the only place in the world and only moment in time that mattered for me, isolated from all past and future moments, this symmetrically aligned target before my eyes: geometrical, hence painless—because geometry is painless, without flesh or even the concept of death—a pure, mental construction, a reassuring abstraction, a single triangle and rectangle, the triangle of ten red and white curved pins arranged before me, the rectangle of the long, almost white lane of natural wood stretched out beneath my feet, smooth and slightly greased, urging me to release my ball and watch it roll, silently, which I did, in slow motion, following it, accompanying it, transporting it with my mind to the end of the lane without thinking about anything else, without even thinking about the death of Marie's father, the lane encouraging me to let go of the thought of this death at last—I had been waiting for more than twenty hours now to stop thinking about the death of Marie's father—watching the ball roll slowly and crash into the pins, knocking all of them down and affording me a brief, and violent, rush of pleasure.

When I turned around, Li Qi was there. I looked up and saw her walking near the bar. She had seen us and was heading toward us, carrying an elegant pink and gray paper bag in her hand (she must have gone shopping), a square-shaped bag from a high-end clothing store, the handles white and decorative, an indecipherable designer label on the side, and small Chinese characters on the front and back. Zhang Xiangzhi got up to greet her, she handed him the bag and he peeked inside—hardly opening it, just enough time to check its contents while protecting it from possible onlookers—and I noticed then an expression of gratitude on his face, of utter thankfulness and near relief. He told her something, and they laughed, and I watched them walk slowly toward me chatting and stopping at the edge of the polished bowling floor. I looked at them, and I wondered for a brief moment what was in the bag. Zhang Xiangzhi set it down on a seat, covering it with his motorcycle helmet, and it wasn't until a few minutes later that I was able to make out the label on the side of the bag, in white letters all strung together, in Roman characters but with the *A*s in the shape of Greek deltas: SAKURAYA (not a clothing line, as I'd initially thought, but the name of a large chain of Japanese consumer electronics stores). I greeted Li Qi from a distance, then Zhang Xiangzhi and I picked our game up where we'd left off, Li Qi sitting down on one of the orange plastic seats reserved for bowlers at the foot of the bowling floor, watching us play in silence. We had just finished our first game and were getting ready to start another when Li Qi got up and headed over to the bar, turning around to ask me, without uttering a word, to join her. It was nothing more than a meeting of the eyes, a shared, mutually intent look, which we may have held a second too long—inconspicuous in the end, yet explicit, filled with significance and a secret pleasure.

Night falls, in China, on faces and shoulders, in sheets of green light, often raw and violent, sometimes sweet and welcoming. The small neon signs of beer companies and brands of liquor, with their white and violet letters, glowed in the semidarkness of the bar, above shelves lined with endless bottles of alcohol and a disparate array of glasses. Li Qi had sat down on a barstool at the counter, and I joined her, I was standing behind her in the semidarkness. She ordered a cocktail (a specific cocktail that only seemed available upon special request, requiring an exact admixture of drops and dashes, a precise mix of alcohols and colors: green, white, amber). She turned her back to me, placed her cigarette in the ashtray on the counter, and, reaching behind her back, offered me her hand. This gesture was made with the utmost simplicity and naturalness, and I could have responded with the same naturalness, the same simplicity, I could have taken her hand and sat down next to her and ordered a cocktail for myself as well. But I didn't move, and I continued to stare at her hand reaching for me in the semidarkness, her delicate fingers spread slightly and her wrist gracefully arched.

My heart began to race at the mere sight of this outstretched hand. Standing behind her, I couldn't see the expression on her face, I could only see her profile outlined against the green light of a billiard lamp, the clear skin of her neck on which gleamed that miniscule piece of jade, casting off occasional glints and circular sparks. She hadn't looked at me, she hadn't turned toward me when she offered me her hand (nor after, nor at any point), she continued to talk to the bartender without paying me the least attention, there was a perfect dichotomy to her attitude, her body and head directed at the bartender (to whom she continued to speak in Chinese), but her right hand still outstretched in the air behind her, an offering, immobile, obstinate, waiting for me to take hold of it, grab it, but I didn't move, she knew quite well that I was standing right behind her, a few centimeters from her shoulder, she could feel the unseen presence of my body at her back, and she had to be waiting for me to take her hand, but I was incapable of moving, I continued to stare at her hand, motionless, on the verge of grabbing it to put an end to the mounting tension, to feel the touch of her skin against my palm and give in to its sweetness—as if letting go were the only act I was capable of—but I didn't budge, in the end I was just as stubborn as Li Qi, as obstinate in my refusal as she was in her perseverance, I stood motionless in the green half-light of the bar, paralyzed, in a daze, and she remained there on her barstool, insistent, majestic, haughty, and almost indifferent—Marie, it suddenly occurred to me, it was one of Marie's gestures—offering me her outstretched hand, openly and publicly, for all eyes in the bowling alley to see.

But perhaps not, perhaps the whole scene went unnoticed by everyone except me—even by Li Qi herself, who seemed to forget it almost immediately, making it disappear as one re-winds a video tape before erasing it—she lifted her cigarette from the ashtray and acted as if nothing had happened. We walked back to our lane together (smiling, we even exchanged a few words about the clear lagoon-like color of her cock-tail), and I had the feeling—perhaps unfounded—that Zhang

Xiangzhi had become aware of something. He was waiting for me by the lane as I went to grab my ball. If, earlier, I had been playing as though there were nothing much at stake in our match, playing with an intense amount of concentration so as to allow me to abstract myself from the world, so as to create another world more to my liking, with the comfort of lines and the stillness of angles, now, however, this was no longer the case. I was playing to win, I was playing to beat Zhang Xiangzhi—and I would beat him, I could feel this fact pulsing in my blood. He had gotten more worked up himself, since I'd returned from the bar with Li Qi. Between turns, he'd chew nervously on the dragon's claw that hung from his neck and bite his lip as he looked up at the screen to check the score, he was less confident, and now, repeatedly, he'd at look at me with a cold, perplexed expression, as if, interrogating my every move, he were trying to make sense of some enigma. Little by little, he had begun to fall into a cold streak, even throwing a few gutter balls. And it wasn't a coincidence that he had started to lose his edge precisely when I'd begun to challenge him, to battle him, because the match had now taken on the appearance of a duel, Li Qi's presence created a rivalry we couldn't ignore, a heated competition, a cold and violent pressure we couldn't escape—Li Qi, whether we liked it or not, had become, symbolically, what was at stake in our increasingly intense match. I focused my eyes on the target—unblinking, tense, locked straight ahead, boring into the pins—and, mentally, I executed a smooth, long, agile movement of the arm, without giving any thought to its outcome. Coordinating the hand with the eye is all it takes—the secret of perfect form. It all comes down to precision; the rest is pathos. I had gotten up to take my turn, Zhang Xiangzhi still held a slight lead. I stood motionless before the lane, my ball poised at face level, I could touch its surface with my lips, I could smell the faint odor of polyurethane emanating from its warm circumference. I moved forward swinging one arm back and released the ball into the lane, it got off to a great start, straight and powerful, I followed its course closely, it reached the front pin with the full force of my throw intact and, as though swept by an invisible wave of energy, tumbling into one another, all the pins fell, all except a single pin, in the corner, still standing, trembling in front of my eyes, wobbling, but refusing to go down. The black mechanical pinsetter slowly descended onto the lane and cleared away the fallen.

I hadn't turned around, I hadn't exchanged a single look with Zhang Xiangzhi. I could sense he was watching me, I could feel his eyes on my back. I had to go again, I felt absolutely impelled to knock down that last pin, I knew that the fate of the match depended on it, and Zhang Xiangzhi knew this just as much as I did. Standing in front of the lane, motionless, eyes focused, I fixed my gaze on the single remaining pin at the far right-hand corner of the lane, I concentrated on it with all my might, and, breathing slowing, patiently, I was trying to clear my mind of all thoughts, to relax my wrist and to synchronize my breathing with the passing seconds, when, suddenly, I heard a noise behind me—a barely audible sound, vibrating, repetitive, as if muffled by the thickness of fabric—the sound of a cell phone ringing in Zhang Xiangzhi's shirt pocket. I turned around, heart racing, already aware that this ringing cell phone was the harbinger of tragedies and disasters, and I watched Zhang Xiangzhi as if in a dream or nightmare remove the phone from his pocket, and then, without flinching, without betraying any expression of pain, or surprise, or fear, he was already up and running toward me, coming to punch me in the face—I don't know, I didn't understand what he wanted from me—his eyes wild, he grabbed me by the arm and pulled me off the bowling floor. In a panic, I dropped my ball, which fell at my feet, heavily, accompanied by the most taboo thud imaginable in a bowling alley—it was as if it had fallen on the marble floor of a cathedral, and the sound of its impact resounded in all our heads, an infinite reverberation that filled and shook each and every atom of the atmosphere of the alley.

All the matches around us had come to a sudden halt, bowlers turned around and were staring at us, frozen, dumbfounded, ball in hand. But we were already far away, we had already left the floor, we'd hardly had the time to grab our things (in my case, my bag, in Zhang's, his SAKURAYA present and his motorcycle helmet) before we were already running past the bar, trailing Li Qi who was urging us to hurry, we were running as fast as possible through the bowling alley, forcing our way through groups of young people who scattered to let us pass, leaving expressions of disbelief and astonishment in our wake, running away toward the exit, running past the shoe counter without being able to get our own shoes back, leaping up the stairs four by four in our bowling shoes, slowed by the waves of people coming down, all of whom we bumped into in passing, finally brought to a halt, caught in a crowd of restaurant-goers waiting outside a small café on the ground floor, finally storming through the crowd with little consideration, shoving people aside, our hearts pounding, to make our way through the mob. Zhang Xiangzhi was the fastest, and he kept turning back to scream something to Li Qi in Chinese, an order or imprecation, with the pink and gray SAKURAYA bag held tightly to his chest, which he had folded and balled up in his hands, a tiny bag with a total volume of less than a liter being much easier for him to protect, but I knew then, was certain, seeing him protect that bag like a baby against his chest, I knew then without the least bit of doubt that the bag contained twenty-five thousand dollars worth of pure heroin or cocaine, or some other kind of narcotic or toxic substance, something white and extremely concentrated, I couldn't say powdery, maybe slimy or even liquefied—I only saw it later, and only for an instant. What I imagined just then, running (and, later, what I saw with my own eyes, in a flash), was a little compact pouch, no bigger than a bag of flour, of white or gray matter, compressed and wrapped in clear plastic.

I don't know when he found the time to put his helmet on in the stairway but Zhang Xiangzhi was already wearing it when we reached the parking lot, the chin strap swinging and beating against his neck, the bag held tight against his chest, all three of us running out into the heat of the humid night, sprinting, out of breath, panic-stricken, stared at by the groups of young people standing bewildered under the entrance's golden arc of lightbulbs. We raced through the dark parking complex without stopping to catch our breath, running toward the motorcycle parked out in the night, its convex, burgundy gas tank reflecting the white glow of the streetlights and, without speaking, as though we'd known since the beginning of time what we had to do, knowing it instinctively (how else could we have been able to do it unrehearsed?), without saying a word or even looking at each other, we all managed to position ourselves on the bike, to magically interlock our three bodies into an appropriate riding position—Zhang Xiangzhi pushed the bike to get it going and then jumped on, while, at the same time, Li Qi was climbing aboard directly behind him, and I followed suit, getting on behind her, it was instantaneous, and the bike sped off, carrying the three of us into the night—now already ripping through the parking lot at top speed, with Zhang Xiangzhi leaning slightly back, steering with one hand, his other hand occupied with hiding the pink and gray SAKURAYA bag, stuck temporarily between his neck and shoulder, trying to stuff it down his shirt, loosening his collar, unbuttoning it, then, losing patience, ripping it to slide the bag into the gaping hole of his torn shirt, letting it fall down to his stomach, securing it there against his abdomen and the warmth of his skin, feeling it move like a living being, pulsing against his flesh as he drove us out of the lot. He turned around to look back at the scene we'd made, and I turned around too, there was a crowd gathering at the entrance to the bowling alley, I could see people entering and exiting under its golden arc, the silhouettes of young people and security guards whose faces were bathed in the electric blue light of the LAS VEGAS sign, and I could feel my heart pounding in my chest, overcome by fear, by pure terror, by a feeling of panic even more terrifying and irrational given that I was completely ignorant of what or whom we were in the process of running away from so frantically.

We had gotten on the freeway and we were riding through the black night, incapable of seeing anything in the dark aside from the flash of headlights coming at us from every direction, behind us, in front of us, blinding us, freezing us in their beams like frightened rabbits. I had the feeling we were running in place, as if transfixed on the freeway, stationary, riveted to the ground, albeit in a tableau indicative of vertiginous speed, our three bodies being propelled forward by the bike, Zhang Xiangzhi the helmeted figurehead, hunched over the handlebars, hands clasping the grips, chest flat and stomach protruding, the SAKURAYA bag making his shirt swell, Li Qi behind him, clinging to his back, and me with my arms around her waist, our three inclined bodies seeming to belong to a single tricephalous creature, panic-stricken, running away, flattened together on this deafening steel machine, flying through the night amid the uninterrupted roar of its engine, but no, we didn't really seem to be moving away from the place we'd just left nor approaching wherever it was we were headed, we were being held in place under the vaulted sky, the vast curved dome of a celestial summer night, unable to make any progress as headlights surged around us from every direction, blinding us in passing, vertiginous streaks of white or electric-blue light shooting through the night and blurring the horizon.

We were moving through the very substance of the night, through its material, through its color, through the wind that whipped our cheeks and lashed our faces methodically, continually, with intense heat. I wrapped my arms tightly around Li Qi's waist, pressing myself up against her body, my chest against her back, smelling her skin whose sweet odor mixed with the hot night, and the tighter I squeezed her, the more I could feel her, too, take part in this silent embrace, clandestine and cosmic, while pretending to ignore the clear promiscuity of our bodies entwined there on the bike, as if too absorbed with the fury of the wind and the urgency of our escape. Endless white lights flitted by between heaven and earth, the vast summer sky looking like an entire universe or subjective landscape of phosphenes above us, with tiny spots of blue and red electric lights blinking steadily, tracing patterns of squiggly dotted lines, and I stopped watching the road, the trees, the straight white lines painted on the asphalt, stopped looking at the sky and the stars, I had taken Li Qi's hand in mine and I was holding it tightly, I was running away with her, running away with her hand in my hand, in this night, in this moment, motionless and without end.

We had reached Beijing (or perhaps we'd never left Beijing) and its multiple circular beltways, its vast, labyrinthine ribbons of elevated freeways, and we traveled down a narrow road suspended in the air and protected on either side by high crash barriers, beyond which the silhouettes of darkened buildings, bridges, and parks could be seen. We were flying straight ahead, but the bike was continually thrown off balance by our cumulative weight, and Zhang Xiangzhi tried to compensate for this by speeding up, gripping the handlebars tightly to brave the wind, which attacked in sudden sideswipes and caused us to wobble over the road for moments at a time. A covered truck would roar past us once in a while, its tarp, badly attached, flapping frantically in the night like a gray, wind-struck sail, and we'd suddenly find ourselves caught in its backwash, pushed toward one of the crash barriers, forced to make a few abrupt swerves before struggling to get back into our lane. Li Qi would lean forward from time to time and, screaming in Chinese, offer a quick suggestion to Zhang Xiangzhi, but he couldn't hear her: her shouts soared off behind us in the night—weightless entreaties borne away by the wind.

Then, coming from far away, but gaining ground, I could hear the sound of police sirens approaching, still in the distance, almost abstract, but coming toward us inexorably, the wailing becoming louder and louder, expanding in the air, possibly even originating from several different sirens, maybe from a convoy of police cars, and so we tried to accelerate even more, but the bike continued to move in place, we had demanded more from it than it had to offer, all it did was start making choking noises like some kind of bad home-repair job, these increasing in volume, a furious hacking, along with the already deafening throb of the engine and the screaming of its exhaust pipe—but the sound of sirens was catching up to us, swooping down on us, and I expected to see flashing blue lights appear behind us at any moment, passing us and blinding our six startled eyes in the night. We turned off the freeway to escape our pursuers, braking to take an off-ramp, but the sirens kept following us, seeming to multiply in space, coming from everywhere at once, as when a number of police cars converge on the scene of an accident at high speed, and then, when I was fully expecting to see the somber sky swept by flashing blue lights, a procession of red lights appeared instead, just as we reached an intersection. We'd found a bustling street of crab and crawfish restaurants, their awnings illuminated by hundreds of red paper lanterns—round, creased, wrinkled, luminous points that seemed alive, their lights twisting, reflected in every direction, blurring across the façades like will-o'-the-wisps, all these scattered lights blending together and seeming to accompany our frantic escape with glowing streaks of red light. We flew through this crowded street, both lively and ghostly, as though peopled by shadows and chimeras wandering up and down the sidewalks in rags through the red glow of the semidarkness, abandoning ourselves to the flow of traffic. A police car appeared now—the first that I'd actually seen—but siren-less, and with all its lights off, looking rather spectral, the hood and windows blanketed by murky reflections, its occupants invisible to outside observers. Zhang Xiangzhi was forced to slow down to let it pass, then stopped violently to avoid a stray dog, white, skeletal, and furless, that took its time crossing the street in front of us, and, squeezing Li Qi's hand a little harder in mine as we crept past the police car, I could feel, physically, mixed with gusts of warm wind against my face, our own breaths spiraling in the air, almost visible, over the bike, like an ethereal exudation of fear, a seepage of cold terror, leaving our bodies to join the sky or else dissolve into the earth, only to transform into those demons of popular Chinese mythology, casting evil spells, spreading death wherever they go.

Our bodies, in fear, were one, joined together on the motorcycle, all caught in the same momentum, the same posture of flight, of running away, all being propelled in the same direction, startled by the slightest sound or movement and frequently looking behind us in search of our invisible pursuers. We had picked up speed and were tearing down the street when Zhang Xiangzhi suddenly braked again, planting his foot down on the ground, his bowling shoe skidding over the asphalt in a spray of gravel, braking hard while pivoting the bike, the back tire spinning in a controlled sideslip, screeching horribly and instantly filling the air around us with the stench of burnt rubber, then hopping the bike up onto the sidewalk, riding against the current of pedestrians for a stretch of ten or so meters over wobbling planks, then squeezing between two plywood walls before entering an enormous construction zone illuminated by arcs of light shining amid the steady buzz of generators. We slid down a gray sand pile, slowly, braking, sinking into the sand and gravel, giving in under our weight. Only a few people were moving around the site, and there were a few cranes at rest standing between stagnating puddles of water, their surfaces reflecting the moonlight. In the distance, next to earthmovers abandoned in the semidarkness, we could make out the silhouettes of prefabricated workers' huts, their doors open, a few windows framing rectangles of yellow light. We inched past the construction vehicles in their ditches before picking up a little speed on a stretch of flat concrete. Nobody seemed to be paying attention to us, a small group of workers at the foot of a giant sand pile was huddled around a brazier, standing or sitting in the sand, barefoot or wearing boots, helmeted, grilling food on skewers in clouds of thick white smoke, and they hardly turned their heads as we passed by. They didn't appear to be bothered by us in any way; it seemed that there wasn't anybody chasing us after all. We emerged into a bright world at the other end of the construction site, bustling streets and congested alleyways, screams, honks, the atmosphere bubbling with summery excitement, the night hot and welcoming, people seated on restaurant terraces, café tables spilling out of open doors, beers being ordered at bar counters and consumed in the streets by people gathered under trees or sitting directly on the sidewalk in groups—it could have been anywhere in the world, the familiar scene of what happens when a city still heavy from the day's heat begins to cool and its inhabitants enjoy the mild lull afforded by the arrival of night, the union of summer and city, of heat and night.

We came flying out into this world without shifting gears, still rushing ahead, still tense, still in a state of shock, running away, our bodies trembling, still feeling the urge to escape, having trouble controlling the bike, braking, hitting the sidewalk too fast, with too much force, too abruptly, slamming against the curb at full speed and then all three of us spilling onto a café terrace, into the legs of a group of people who were forced to jump out of our way, though we didn't exactly fall over, it was more that the bike began to tip to one side before we caught ourselves with our legs, all three of us simultaneously putting one leg down in anticipation of the fall, and then the three of us pushed back off that leg to reposition the bike, still straddling it, our legs still tangled up with the bike, trying to move forward, unable, finally stuck, getting stared at, not saying anything, not apologizing, straining to dislodge our back wheel from the gutter, and then back on our way, moving down the sidewalk against the current of pedestrians, the three of us positioned on the bike *à l'Italienne* once again, as if riding on a Vespa through the mild night, threading our way in slow motion through laughing crowds and conversations around café tables, riding along the shoulder for a stretch before moving back into the street, trying to accelerate to full speed, then braking abruptly in front of an approaching car after only a few meters, veering back up onto the sidewalk, all three of us giving a push with our feet to get ourselves moving again, to pick up speed, slaloming between tables, traveling down the entirety of the boulevard in this fashion until reaching the end, where there was nothing, no more cafés, no more people, charging forward through the night for a few dozen meters, then braking, stopped once again by a busy street, blocked by a sea of pedestrians flooding the road, a small street of bars and tiny dive restaurants serving food on skewers, much darker, lacking streetlights, only a few white and green neon signs, wooden doors, bamboo blinds letting out hints of shimmering, tawny candlelight, a few storefronts lit up with green bulbs shining behind their glass windows. Zhang Xiangzhi slowed down in front of a bar, didn't park, simply stopped by the entrance to the bar, and he got off the bike while it was still rolling to a halt, all three of us got off the rolling bike, our legs rising in unison, simply leaving the speed-deprived bike alone to tip over there on the sidewalk, and Zhang Xiangzhi, leading the way, still wearing his white helmet, went into the bar first, straining to push the door open, then finally shoving it with his shoulder, knocking away the people who'd been blocking it, and the three of us walked into the bar, clearing a path through the throng of bodies and wooden tables as we tried to make our way to the bar in back, where, in a fog of cigarette smoke shot through by beams from green spotlights, a group of Chinese musicians was performing on a small stage, their long-haired singer seated on a stool, a mike angled at his mouth, the stage surrounded by a dense crowd, all on their feet, bottles of Tsingtao in their hands, and we continued to work our way toward the bar, Zhang Xiangzhi leading the way, determined and aggressive, elbowing, even pushing his way through to clear a path for us while at the same time remaining quiet and polite, covering the distension under his gray shirt with a protective hand, followed by Li Qi who, directly in front of me, kept turning around, grabbing my hand and pulling me forward so as not to lose me in the crowd. When we reached the bar, we went directly behind the counter without even acknowledging the young bartenders, without asking permission, we headed straight to a back room, a miniscule kitchen-space in which an old lady was cooking amid a chaos of stacked beer cases and collapsing shelves, all lit by a single bare lightbulb. Without even glancing at the old lady, Zhang Xiangzhi reached out and grabbed a chair by its back, an old kitchen chair made of flimsy plastic that he set down against the bar counter and then mounted (I was sure it was going to snap under his weight). There he was, behind the bar, in the middle of a concert, standing on a plastic chair that Li Qi was holding steady with both hands, and he opened a hatch in the ceiling, letting it swing down violently, and, with little concern for anything going on around him—the looks he was getting, the concert being performed, or even Li Qi and myself, both watching him from either side of his chair—he dug his hand into his gray shirt, rummaged around, and, with a quick jerk, a brutal expulsion, he extracted the gray and pink SAKURAYA bag from his gut, and, tearing open the bag to get at its precious cargo, stripping away that superfluous protection, letting it fall, empty, down to his feet, he exposed, in the green light of the bar—for the space of a second, a single second, the amount of time necessary to slip it through the hatch—pallid, limp, shriveled, the little package of dead, compact material, white or gray, the size of a fetus compressed in clear plastic.

He closed the hatch, got off the chair, picked it back up, and returned it to the kitchen, and we retraced our steps, we walked out from behind the bar without saying a word to anyone, and weaved our way back through the crowd toward the exit. In the street, still very tense, one of his eyes twitching, he told me to go back to the hotel, to take a taxi and go back to the hotel. *Understand?* he asked, eye still twitching. He picked the bike up off the sidewalk, positioned it so that it was facing the street, and got on with Li Qi. *Money?* he asked before leaving. *Need money?* he asked. I shook my head no, and I watched them ride off. Li Qi turned around and looked at me, they were already far away, lost in traffic among pedestrians and cars. Standing outside the bar, I followed the motorcycle with my eyes and I saw it reach the end of the street—Li Qi was still facing me, still looking at me, she was still looking at me—and vanish.

III

The Mediterranean was as calm as a lake. Its surface was slightly ruffled in a continuous, almost immobile undulation of ripples. I listened to the steady splash of water softly crashing against the boat's hull, the pulse of the sea, the imperceptible lapping of waves. I felt as though I'd been removed from time, as though I was within silence itself—a silence untainted by thought.

I had arrived in Paris in the evening, about twenty hours earlier, unshaven, the white shirt I'd been wearing the previous night stained with filth and fear and sticking to my chest, bearing traces of all its travels: the gray dust of Beijing, microscopic deposits of salt, plaster, and asphalt fossilized in the fabric, scratches from rocks and gravel. It had been softened by the heat, stretched out, loosened, had braved the heavy humidity of the day and the dryness of the night, withstood my cold sweats as well as terrifying blasts of air-conditioning, the sudden glacial gusts pouring out of air vents that had stiffened it like Listral glass in the brutal heat and then the chilliness of my flight from Beijing to Paris. After arriving at Charles de Gaulle, I wandered through the terminal in my bowling shoes and my tattered shirt (that sagging relic, hanging down past my waist and sticking to my chest, stinking of dried sweat), going back and forth between different terminals, moving from one counter to the next, turned away and ignored by indifferent ticket agents who provided me with virtually no information, and grudgingly at that, at best out of ignorance, at worst out of a simple lack of concern—a smiling lack of concern, all the more disconcerting for its courtesy—before I went down to lower levels of the airport to ask questions at further counters, where I finally ended up being helped by a nice female employee who took pity on me in my distressed state and went over the different ways I might be able to continue on to Elba. There were no direct flights from Paris and no registered airports on the island, apart from the one in La Pila that was only for small tourist planes. The usual way, if not the only way, was to fly into Piombino via one city or another, at which point a traveler could reach Elba by means of a succession of ferryboats. Other cities offered slightly more direct routes at certain periods of the year, Civitavecchia, Monte San Savino, Livorno, maybe Genoa too, but it was impossible to get any information on ferry schedules or boat availability at this remove. In the end, my best option was to fly to Piombino via Rome or Florence (it would have been interminable to go by train, and I didn't have the strength to drive), so she and I worked together to get me on a flight to Italy departing that same night—because if I left that night, I still might be able to reach Elba in time to attend Marie's father's funeral.

I found out a little while later, after having called Marie from a pay phone, that the interment would take place around eleven o'clock in the morning, or maybe noon, she didn't know for sure, she didn't feel like talking, it'd be better to call when I got there.

And I was about to arrive. We had cast off from Piombino very early in the dry and limpid air of a sunny morning. As soon as the boat set sail, I took refuge in one of the cabins on the lower deck where there were no other passengers, and, sliding the pleated blue curtain over the window, I began to drift off to sleep in a stiff chair with metal armrests. I hadn't slept for forty-eight hours, or rather I'd been half-asleep for the whole endless, foggy duration of my ongoing, uninterrupted voyage, during whose unvarying hours I could hardly distinguish day from night. I had napped in taxis and minibuses, in transit zones and waiting areas, I had drifted off several times on the plane, I had spent two short restless nights in hotel rooms, but never fully sleeping, never reaching a deep sleep, always on the verge of sleep, never quite able to cross the invisible divide separating true waking from true rest. Even after going back to the hotel, in Beijing, I couldn't sleep, I laid there with my eyes open, staring at the ceiling in the dark, listening for any noise in the hall that might alert me to Zhang Xiangzhi and Li Qi's arrival, but I didn't hear anything, and the following morning, after I'd gotten up at dawn to leave for the airport, I went by their room before going down to the lobby and stood there for a while, my ear against their door, listening, but I didn't hear anything, I didn't hear a single sound in their room, which left me in some doubt, a doubt that continues even now, as to whether they ever came back.

I was still, and I remained for a long time, in that state of suspension one enters while traveling, that intermediary state in which the body, in motion, seems to be making steady progress from one geographical location toward another (like the arrow I'd tracked on the in-flight video screen on my trip back from Beijing, charting the plane's movement over a stylized world map, covered with mountains), but in which the mind, incapable of adapting to this mode of steady and slow transition, is, for its part, unable to keep from splitting its attention between thoughts of the place we've only just departed, and concurrent thoughts of the place we're approaching. During the whole course of my trip, then, I was still in Beijing, but already in Elba at the same time, my mind unable to move from one place to the other as easily as my body, to forget one place so as to focus on the other, stuck instead in the temporary between-ness of the journey, as if this transitory state, extendable and elastic, could be stretched to the point that, in thought, I was nowhere, neither in Beijing nor in Elba, but always outside the borders of either place, always both at rest and in motion, sitting and dozing off with all my emotions and sensations buried inside me (which I could perhaps reawaken later on), not only in the boat carrying me to Elba but also, and simultaneously, in every vehicle I had taken since my initial departure. It was as though this trip were the quintessence of all the trips I'd ever taken in my life, the hundreds of hours spent in planes and trains, in cars and boats, moving from one piece of land to another, from one country to another, from one continent to another, during which my body, motionless, moved through space, but also—inconspicuously, in an imperceptible and insidious manner, furtively, gradually, with distorting, destructive effects—through time. I had felt the passing of time with an acute awareness since the beginning of my trip, all the hours, unvarying, drifting by amid the constant hum of engines, each the same as the next—time, ample and fluid, carrying me along in spite of my immobility, with death (and the wounds left by its claws) the measure of its dark progression.

Since leaving Beijing I'd felt as though it wasn't Marie that I was traveling to see in Elba, but her father, that he was the reason I had decided to make this trip, that he'd be there waiting for me on the quay in Portoferraio, like when he came to pick Marie and I up and drive us to La Rivercina after we'd arrived by boat. We debarked through the hold, Marie in sandals amid the cars and tourist buses, wearing sunglasses and with a large bag slung over her shoulder (often with some tiny, precious package in her hand, like a delicious almond-paste and pine-nut tart from Sampierdarenese di Sabatini & Pilato), rushing excitedly to meet her father on the quay and to celebrate our reunion effusively with hugs and smiles, which, since we were blocking traffic, was soon followed by a concert of honks that brought our warmhearted welcome to an abrupt end. We would meander out of the way and put our suitcases and bags in the bed of her father's old, battered, dusty pickup truck, its ancient license plate marked by an orange "Li" for "Livourne," the other letters half effaced, setting the bags down among loose hay and old blankets, gas cans, tools, saddles, harnesses, stirrups, and then all three of us would squeeze in together on the torn seats in the front, their springs exposed—Marie between her father and I, imperturbable, her sweet from Sampierdarenese di Sabatini & Pilato in her hand, held by its knotted ribbon as though it were a valuable hatbox from Dolce & Gabbana—before driving away in the direction of La Rivercina.

Her father's property, La Rivercina, was located in an isolated and undeveloped area on the northeast part of the island, near the beaches of Nisporto and Nisportine (between Rio Marina and Cavo). The house was surrounded by trees, oaks, olive trees, a few orange and lemon trees, some coastal shrubs, and a large fenced-in area for his horses. For the past decade, her father had been spending the whole year at La Rivercina. He'd kept his small apartment in Paris, but spent less and less time there, he'd become solitary and reclusive, and he soon developed the habit of leaving Elba only in the summer, precisely when all the Parisian tourists would arrive. He lived alone, secluded, with his horses, garden, a little stretch of submarine pasture, solitary walks, and a remarkable library of art history and philosophy books, his ties to the world becoming more and more tenuous as he cultivated a mild form of misanthropy, having become convinced that the less contact one has with others, the better one's relationship with them is likely to grow. He had fixed up an old stone house on an overgrown part of his property for Marie, an ancient garden pavilion that he'd restored, doing most of the work himself, the stonework as well as the woodwork, before starting on the painting. That's probably where Marie was right now, in the old stone house that her father had fixed up for her, or else on the first floor of the main building, silent, with its majestic dark-wood furniture and waxed floors that smelled like polish and scented wax, alone in the vast and empty house, blinds closed and curtains drawn, with her dead father on the second floor, the mortician's work finished, lying supine on the bed, hair combed, hands joined, in a suit and tie, and Marie in the library, silent, curled up in one of the large straight-backed chairs, looking at the books on the library's shelves, or else in the garden, leaning over the clay pots filled with herbs, thyme, sage, rosemary, kneeling in the moist, soft soil of the stone-enclosed garden and pensively reattaching one end of a frayed string that her father must have used to tie the fuzzy stem of a tomato plant to the stick that was supporting it, and I was suddenly overcome by a strong feeling of tenderness for Marie, not only of compassion, but simply of love.

The coast of Elba was in sight. I had gone out on deck and was watching Portoferraio unfurl in the distance, still a shimmering mass of orange roofs indistinguishable from one another in the liquid light of the morning. The city was gradually gaining definition, beginning to stand out among the mountains and neighboring hillsides, the contours of bell towers and houses coming into focus as we got closer to shore. The ferry's engines slowed, and presently we were drifting alongside the rocky headland of the old town, I could almost have reached out and touched it, its green-shuttered houses arrayed in a gradation of colors from ochre to pale yellow to pink, its sloping streets disappearing behind the walls of the city's ramparts. With the engines humming softly, we skirted the shore of Fort Stella and began to enter the harbor. The ferry, still moving, still propelled by the impetus of its passage—the proportions of the boat out of place in this new company, much taller and wider than the modern buildings and the few cafés of the port, toward which we were still drifting—seemed, for a second, at the moment of docking, to be intent on continuing onto land, joining the buildings of the port. I felt the light thud of the hull hitting some nearby buoys, which threw me off balance on deck and made the boat rock for a moment by the quay. People were already starting to move below decks, deckhands were tossing mooring lines to be tied to pontoons now that we'd reached the quay. Leaning over the rail, I watched the few people scattered around the deserted quay, hoping in vain to spot Marie, searching for her, for her father too, next to the little harbormaster's office, there where he'd been waiting so often when he'd come to pick us up, but there was nothing to see, Marie wasn't there and her father was dead.

I couldn't find a taxi when I got off the ferry, so I started off on foot among the debarking cars crowding the quay. I wasn't planning on staying at La Rivercina on this trip, I was thinking about getting a room in Portoferraio and not calling Marie until I'd gotten settled in somewhere. I had left the harbor and was walking in the sun in search of a hotel, strolling through deserted streets along the sea, crossing vacant lots and parking lots and small silent plazas with dry fountains. The town seemed abandoned at this early afternoon hour, people must have been at the beach, there was no one to be found in the streets or sitting on the public benches, only a solitary Vespa zooming by from time to time, fading away down an empty road before vanishing altogether. I had entered the old town now, I climbed up the silent, flower-lined streets whose stairs led up to Fort Falcone. Bougainvilleas fell in showers from the terraces, and sometimes, passing a tiny alley, I saw the rough ledge of a rampart looking over a cliff and out onto the sunlit sea.

I ended up finding a hotel near the city center, a beautiful old building with a terrace and green shutters. I walked up the steps at the entrance and crossed through an arbor under which white tableclothed tables had been set for breakfast. I went into the dark, deserted bar, and I walked along the counter and through a glass door that led to a sort of reception area in which, behind another little wooden counter, there was a corkboard hanging with some room keys attached. I called out, but got no response. I walked over to the stairs and went up a few steps to look around on the second floor. A door opened below me, and a lady wearing a chef's apron appeared in the hall, welcoming, voluble, kind, smiling brightly, and she told me that the hotel was completely booked (*mi dispiace ma siamo al completo*). She seemed sincerely sorry (*ma in agosto, se non c'è gente in agosto*), and, keeping me from leaving (*è piena stagione, capisce*), she told me to wait one moment, pondering something conspicuously (whenever she wasn't speaking, she seemed compelled to act out each of her unspoken words as demonstratively as possible), her hand raised, held in the air, didactic, instructing me to wait patiently. She told me to follow her and went to get a key from the kitchen, led me through a hall whose floor was tiled in stone. We exited the hotel from the rear, crossed a small yard where there was a swing, a small inflatable swimming pool made of blue plastic, and some shovels and red rakes strewn around, passed through a small courtyard where laundry was hung up to dry, and at last reached an isolated pavilion whose door she opened with the key she carried. Through the door was a large room, shaded and cool, with a steel bed frame and an oatmeal-colored bedspread and a sliding glass door that opened out onto a small vegetable garden. She asked me if this would work for me, the shower and toilets could be found outside. I said yes, that it was great. I didn't even wait for her to leave before I picked up the phone on the nightstand to call La Rivercina.

I let the phone ring for a while, but nobody picked up. I wanted to try Marie on her cell phone, but, to reach her cell phone, I had to make a long-distance call, and I found out then, after getting a busy signal several times, that long-distance calls couldn't be made from this room. I told the lady I had to make a long-distance call, it was an emergency. She looked at me, a little surprised, even suspicious, but still with goodwill, and together we went to the front desk. She led me through the large hotel restaurant adjoining the terrace and handed me the old gray rotary phone from the counter. I dialed Marie's number. I could hear it ringing, I held my breath, and finally I heard someone pick up. Marie, I said in a soft voice. She didn't respond right away, then, in a shaky voice, a fragile voice, very faint and hardly audible, unrecognizable—as though she were cold, trembling—she told me that she couldn't speak to me right now, that it wasn't possible. She asked me where I was, and I told her at a hotel in Portoferraio. There was a pause, she didn't say anything, didn't respond, something must have diverted her attention, and then I heard the faint sound of church bells on the phone and, while I heard it on the phone, I could also hear it in the street, a slow tolling of bells, continual, lugubrious, not far away, outside, in the street, I looked over at the terrace and tried to see it out in the sunlit street, the church had to be less than a hundred meters from the hotel—but I wasn't able to see it from where I was—and I realized then that the solemn notes reverberating in the silence around me were from the funeral knell tolling for Marie's father.

When I was finally allowed to go out onto the terrace (the lady in the apron had detained me at the front desk until I could fill out my registration information), I realized that the cathedral of Portoferraio was indeed less than a hundred meters from the hotel. Its doors had been shut and the church square was deserted, its stone-covered ground saturated with white light, shining in the sun and reflecting this glow back up onto the church's façade. There were no signs of mourning anywhere outside the cathedral, no funeral veils or crêpe shawls, no wreaths or even flowers aside from a few earthenware pots of oleander which must have been a permanent church-front decoration. The bells had fallen silent now, nobody was in the square, nothing indicated that a funeral was going on inside the church. I had left the hotel and was walking toward the square when I noticed a hearse parked a little off to the side, under a plane tree, not even in front of the church, in a parking lot with other vehicles, between tourist cars and campers.

When I opened the creaking door of the church, I was welcomed by the scent of burning candles and cool marble. I stopped at the threshold, struck by the heavy silence and welcoming atmosphere reigning inside. I remained still for a moment, I could hear, as if coming from a great distance, the whispering voice of an invisible priest resonating through the nave. It wasn't long before my eyes became accustomed to the darkness and I was able to make out around twenty people seated on old wooden pews. I passed silently between two pillars and stopped in a side aisle, toward the back, under a large religious painting that, despite its faded colors, demanded attention in the half-light. And that's when I noticed the coffin in front of the altar. Marie was alone before the coffin, standing erect in a white shirt and tight-fitting beige pants, a cold look on her face, impassive, solemn, her countenance betraying a certain degree of stubbornness. When she saw me, finally recognized me, she looked at me as if defeated, a wave of sadness swept across her face, but she immediately regained her composure, and again became cold, dignified, distant, she only gestured to me to sit down somewhere on a back pew, but not next to her, she wasn't telling me to join her. The coffin was placed on a rudimentary catafalque before the altar; a single bouquet of wild island flowers adorned the brass crucifix inlaid in the varnished wood of the coffin's lid. Further back, a funeral wreath of foxtail lilies and white snapdragons hung around a sandstone chalice, which stood on a silver platter whose surface reflected the near-unearthly light of a red and blue stained-glass window. The officiating priest was surprisingly young, wearing glasses, standing in front of Marie in his cream silk chasuble and officiating in Italian with a reedy voice and an intonation that prolonged each syllable (*per il cristiano, la morte è consunzione, il compimento del suo battesimo, in verità si tratta della rinascita già annunciata nel primo sacramento*). His gestures were smooth, his wrists graceful, he wore a green silk stole around his neck and addressed the attendees in a delicate voice, feminine, speaking to a crowd essentially composed of old ladies dressed in black, with, here and there, extravagant touches of night-blue, violet, or turquoise, and I figured that it was probably the regular Sunday mass attendees of the Portoferraio cathedral, who were only attending the funeral for Marie's father by chance—otherwise there would only have been the two of us in the church, Marie and myself, paying our respects to her father. Three of us, counting Maurizio, I also recognized Maurizio among the attendees, looking solemn in a pale blue and black checkered shirt, black pants, and suspenders, an elegant hat held in his crossed hands, and he sat directly behind Marie, but at a respectable distance, two or three rows behind her, his hair gray, skin thick and wrinkled, weathered slightly by time, yet with a strong, sturdy build for someone in his eighties.

I was looking at Marie, alone in this unknown church, standing in front of her father's coffin—Marie determinedly unflinching, filling the entire space of the church with her imposing presence—Marie with her chin held high before her father's coffin in what seemed to be, the more I looked, the more closely I observed, nothing more or less than equestrian attire—white shirt, skin-tight riding pants, and knee-length, black leather boots—Marie, in equestrian attire before her father's coffin, with a frozen face, impassive, solemn, watching the priest while stubbornly suppressing her pain, a feeling of pain mixed with anger and exhaustion, her lips pursed, as though she had a riding crop in her hand, a whip, ready to strike out, to beat someone, to lash the stifling air of the church, and it struck me then how much she looked like her father, to what degree she had inherited his intransigence, his temper, his compulsiveness, and I realized then, or at least I could imagine, how the extravagant idea of showing up to her father's funeral in equestrian attire had occurred to her. She must have gotten up at dawn this morning, Marie had woken up at dawn because she knew that the funeral-home people would come for the body in the early morning, that they'd be at La Rivercina no later than eight, and she had gotten dressed with meticulous attention, for her father's sake, she was all done up, her hair pulled back, her makeup carefully applied, and when Maurizio had welcomed the four darkly dressed funeral-home personnel at the gate of the garden, she hadn't said a word to them, she had disappeared into the house, she didn't want to see the preparation of the body, the struggle to bring the coffin down the stairs, didn't want to watch it carried through the garden and slid into the hearse, but, when the cortège was ready, when all the doors had been slammed shut before they headed out, Marie was there again, on horseback, waiting for the hearse at the entrance to the property. She had saddled up one of her father's mares, and, in one of those sudden acts of madness she was always capable of, an act of flamboyance, of audacity and bravura, Marie, who never got on a horse, who was by no means a frequent rider, had escorted the hearse from La Rivercina all the way to Portoferraio to pay her final respects to her father, she had led the hearse through the deserted streets of Elba across the dozen or so kilometers that separate La Rivercina from Portoferraio, but, unaccustomed to riding horses, not being a frequent rider, she had kept the horse to a slow walk for the whole dozen-kilometer stretch, tugging the reins to keep it at a slow pace, not letting the hearse pass her, forcing the driver to follow in her wake and to drive slowly so as to not frighten the animal, ambling in this way through all the streets of Elba in the early morning with the long black hearse behind her and the sea below, calm and slack in the glistening sun. The cortège progressed slowly through the smell of a hot horse, of dew, and of death. Marie, sitting erect in the saddle in her immaculate shirt, staring straight ahead with pride and dignity, her eyes sparkling with exaltation, rode on in the sun with a feeling of omnipotence, of timelessness. The slow and silent cortège passed vineyards and wild island shrubs, proceeding around the ruins of a Roman villa from the Imperial era, vestiges of its walls standing in sun-soaked fields, black mosaics weathered by time and crumbling among the tall grass, the bramble, the strawberry and mastic trees. Soon the cortège reached the city, the streets became wider and busier, but Marie didn't cut across the fields to get to the port, she stayed right in the middle of the four-lane street, the long hearse with tinted windows still behind her, which, having become docile, like her horse, no longer tried to pass her, was being kept to a walking pace, coaxed along, following her slowly, rolling ahead with its engine humming, and so she entered the city, escorting her dead father on horseback through the deserted streets of Portoferraio, passing through the Viale Alcide Gasperi, through the Via Carioli, crossing the Viale Alessandro Manzoni, where a few rare café-goers had come out onto the sidewalk to see the cortège pass, watching it vanish slowly out of sight on its way to the port. Marie had crossed the Piazza Citti and entered the Via Vittorio Emanuele II, probably at the same time that my ferry had come within sight of Portoferraio, and she must have seen me on the deck then, returning like her to Portoferraio for her father's funeral, and our spirits, for a split second, must have met in mutual grief and respect, uniting and becoming one in the clear blue sky.

I'm not sure when Marie noticed my absence from the church—since I was no longer in the church—if it was during the service itself, turning around to look for me and suddenly finding nothing but an empty space between the marble columns where I had been standing a few minutes earlier—an emptiness immediately tangible, abnormal, a cold emptiness, silent, disquieting—or if it wasn't until later that she became aware of my absence, when the church doors had been opened at the end of the service, letting the sunlight penetrate the interior of the church, a great wave of bright light penetrating the semidarkness and flooding the marble floor of the church. It may have been at that moment that my absence had begun to worry her, my failure to join her by the coffin, while the other attendees started to go their separate ways outside the church, or maybe even later, while she was receiving condolences, inside the church itself, at the top of the stairs of the sacristy, struggling to listen to the comforting words of people who had come up to give her a hug, while, peering anxiously over their shoulders, she looked for me but didn't find me anywhere in the church, squeezing Maurizio tightly in her arms, not letting go, the only one who understood and loved her.

Marie had reached the cemetery by foot, the mare by her side, which she led by the reins, accompanied by the priest and a choirboy in a white alb. The horse followed her obediently through the streets of Portoferraio, its nostrils moist, ears pointed, curious and inquisitive. The cemetery was two kilometers from the city, slightly uphill, a village cemetery with no more than twenty headstones. It was located at the end of a curve of a coastal road, near the edge of a steep cliff, the entrance was protected by a rusted iron gate whose recalcitrant doors had been opened in advance by the funeral-home people, waiting now for the cortège outside the cemetery walls. Three workers were waiting there in silence, all dressed in similar dull gray suits, blue shirts, black ties, the eldest wore a chauffeur's cap embroidered with decorative, golden initials, and the two younger men, serious, mute, wore sunglasses with the top button of their shirts unbuttoned, their ties loosened, all three of them watching the hearse struggle to enter the cemetery in reverse, skidding on the gravel as it accelerated to make it up the last few meters of the rocky incline. The driver had stuck his head out the window, and the other workers were directing him with terse hand gestures. The hearse continued in reverse up the cemetery's sole road and slowed at the open grave, shaking for a moment as it braked, from front bumper to rear, the body of the car burning in the hot air, before finally coming to a stop, majestic and out of place, a long black limousine gleaming under the cypress trees, outlined against the calm sea. Marie, who hadn't arrived at the cemetery yet, she'd taken a different road, suddenly appeared at the top of the hill holding a red bucket. Marie had tied her mare to a tree by the road, she had climbed up the little hill and had led the horse through coastal shrubs, scratching her arms and thighs in passing, and had tied its reins as well as she could around a wild olive tree, then walked back down to get a bucket from the cemetery, which she filled up at a small wall faucet. She had brought it back to the horse and let him drink directly from the bucket to quench his thirst—he lapped up the water without pausing for breath.

A small group of about ten people were present at the cemetery when the funeral-home men took the coffin out of the hearse. They hoisted it up on their shoulders carefully and then set it down flat in the ready grave. Outside the stone walls of the cemetery, one could see, beyond the silent crowns of the cypresses, the immense blue sea, dotted by still white sails and the thin streaks of foam left by passing yachts like ephemeral scars on the water. The priest, standing at the foot of the grave, his green stole around his neck, offered a few last words before lowering the coffin. Marie stepped forward to touch the coffin for the last time and, placing her hand flat against its surface, she felt the smooth surface of the varnished wood with her fingers. Then the funeral-home men stepped forward, and the coffin disappeared from her sight forever.

Marie, alone, walked off. Maybe she'd asked Maurizio to take the horse back to La Rivercina, or maybe she'd handed it over to someone else, but she left the cemetery on foot and without company. She walked listlessly in the sun, going down a small seaside path that led to the city, staring off into space, much sadder now that there was nothing left to take care of for the funeral, no more decisions to make, nothing to do and nowhere to go. It probably didn't occur to her immediately, but the unassuageable pain that had been causing her to feel as though she were plunging down an endless abyss, all her passiveness and dejection, presently began to transform into a diffuse fear provoked by my absence. Her thoughts then focused on my disappearance from the church, trying to make sense of it, understand it, trying to find reasons for it in order to avoid confronting the real source of her pain. I became the person responsible for her suffering, I was the one who was tormenting her, without my even doing anything—my presence alone was making her suffer, and my absence even more so—me, the one who wasn't there when she needed me, not in Paris when she found out that her father had died, not in Elba when she arrived, when all the practical details of the funeral had to be arranged, the one who, after having finally showed up, this morning, at the church, had immediately disappeared, before talking to her, before saying a single word to her, before kissing her and holding her in my arms, before sharing her pain, depriving her of my presence at the same time as making it flicker in front of her, causing her to tremble, giving her the chills, just as I always did.

Marie had reached Portoferraio and was walking through the deserted city toward the harbor. She was wandering aimlessly, she didn't know where she was going, she was passing through small streets, tripping over uneven cobblestones, and looking at the flowers of tiny fenced-in gardens alongside houses with sea views, at bougainvilleas, oleanders, and hollyhock. The streets were deserted, with a few stylized *T*s here and there, white on a black background, incomprehensible and haunting, on the signs of closed tobacconists' shops. Marie had hoped to run into me right away, sitting on the steps of a fountain or a church, or suddenly appearing after turning a street corner, but finally gave up on finding me at all, still with the same sense of anxiety filling her chest, the same diffuse fear, heavy, gravid, expanding every second, at last reaching a point where she could even begin to wonder, no longer trusting her senses, if she'd ever actually seen me in the church in the first place, if it was really me she had seen between the church's marble columns, or if, only seeing what she had wanted to see, it wasn't just a hallucination, if, in reality, I wasn't still in China, or still on my way back, and only in Elba in spirit.

Marie began looking for me again, frantically now, stopping outside café windows to peer through the glass between her cupped hands to see if I was inside. After searching through the half-light of the interior, she'd start back on her way, crossing abandoned courtyards and marketplaces whose premises, filled with old wooden crates and the remains of rotting vegetables, had been taken over by pigeons and cats. My absence was like an additional wound, an invisible and relentless feeling of unease, of ceaseless anxiety. She'd walk on and then turn back around, wander through sunlit squares with dark thoughts filling her head, at times thoughts of disappearance, of fear and death, at others of exaltation, promising herself that if she could find me before the end of the hour, she'd go into a church and convince the priest to ring the bells in celebration of our reunion.

Marie was hot, she was thirsty, she went into cafés and had espressos at their counters, staring off into space, sometimes finishing the little glass of warm water offered with her coffee. She hadn't really eaten anything for two days, incapable of consuming any food apart from ice cream, just buying herself cones, one after another, which simultaneously cooled her down and made her feel even more dehydrated. She'd have a barista shuffling back and forth behind the counter and the refrigerated display case outside the café while she took her time selecting a flavor, which she'd point to despite remaining undecided, then change her mind even though the barista had already scooped the ice cream into a cone, making him take it out so she could choose another flavor, replacing strawberry with pistachio, changing her mind again, she didn't know anymore, asking the barista's opinion (*e la stracciatella, è buona la stracciatella*?), who, ice-cream scoop in hand, stood waiting (what angelic patience), asking him for advice but not listening to it, becoming herself again for a brief moment, impossible, unique, irresistible.

Marie had left the café and was finishing her ice cream in the street, it was melting in the sun and dripping onto her hands, forcing her to stop and rotate the cone and lick the edges in order to contain the spillage. A few years back Marie had invented a line of designer ice cream dresses that would melt off models' bodies leaving liquid streaks on their bare skin, old rose and tobacco colored. It became one of her emblematic creations, that ephemeral collection, an Archimboldoesque spring-summer line of ice creams, sherbets, granitas, frulatti, and frappés that would melt down the naked skin of her models, dripping from their shoulders and streaming down the curves of their hips, their skin covered with goose-bumps and their nipples hardened by the coldness. Marie had wed bare flesh and invisible fabrics, blending ingredients and materials, sugar, milk, flour, syrups, a little lace, a little bit of transparent silk, a little gauze and gold thread to attach the ice cream to the bodies, an extravagant array of colors and flesh tones, mango, lemon, mandarin, peach, melon, finishing with more sanguine shades, stormier colors so as to mourn the end of summer, tragic sorbets, dark and crepuscular, mauve and black, cassis, blue and blackberry.

Marie ended up at the old port, and the sun struck her with a new intensity as she stepped out of a little covered passageway into the violent white light that was beating down on the paving stones of the harbor (she wanted to put on her sunglasses, but realized she was already wearing them). Blinking her eyes, blinded by the light, she began to walk along the quay. A few yachts were anchored in the sun, attached to pontoons, bobbing among the red and white buoys that dotted the water. She paused to look at a guy showering in his boat with a hose, hairy and plump, wearing tight bathing shorts, joyously applying soap to his hair and inside his shorts. His wife was tanning across from him on the deck, still as marble, one knee bent and an arm covering her face, a young-looking older woman, emaciated, who, between her trim physique and waxen immobility, looked like a work of hyperrealism. Marie watched them for a moment before continuing on her way. There was a little more activity going on at the old port now, busy cafés whose white-cloth awnings stretched over terraces, a few tourists here and there eating ice cream out of glasses adorned with miniature paper parasols, crinkled and pale. Some souvenir shops selling flippers, snorkels, and a selection of multicolor beach towels had also opened, likewise welcoming tourists. Marie had reached the end of the quay, which ended in a cul-de-sac in front of the Linguella Museum of Archeology. She pushed her sunglasses up on her forehead and turned around in every direction to look for me. But where was I?

Marie remembered then that I had mentioned a hotel to her (she couldn't remember the name, or I hadn't told her, or she hadn't listened, but she was sure that I had mentioned a hotel to her), and she began going into hotels to ask at the front desk if someone had come to reserve a room this morning. The receptionists' responses varied drastically, at times straightforward and cordial (simply telling her no, nobody had reserved a room this morning), at other times standoffish, as, giving them my name and trying to describe me, she'd receive suspicious looks or silent turns of their head, as though they were hiding something from her, which only worked to intensify her anxiety. She passed like this from hotel to hotel, going up dark narrow stairs only to reach deserted entresols, venturing into tiny courtyards sweltering in the sun as she followed makeshift, handwritten signs indicating available rooms only to be turned away by old ladies with barking dogs who'd hardly even crack open their windows to answer her questions. No, nobody had seen me in Portoferraio, nobody had seen this faceless man whom she tried to describe with her faltering voice.

When, going down the steps of the Salita Cosimo dei Medici, Marie caught sight of the Hotel Albergo l'Ape Elbana, she knew at once that that's where I was, behind its thick façade and closed blinds. At the front desk, the lady listened to her attentively, nodding her head in sympathy. Yes, she certainly had seen me that morning. Yes, I had come to ask for a room around eleven o'clock (she opened a drawer and took out my registration form, which she showed Marie). I had even come by again a little later, I had come to the front desk to ask for a bath towel and find out how the hot water in the shower worked. Since then she hadn't seen me, maybe I had gone back out, or maybe I was still in my room, my key wasn't at the front desk. The lady accompanied Marie to the small yard and pointed to the little pavilion further back. Marie walked through the deserted yard. The whitewashed pavilion didn't have any windows looking out onto the yard, yet Marie felt as though she were being watched, she noticed that one of the windows of the main building was slightly open, that there was someone there at the window, probably a hotel guest in his room getting ready to take a nap, a bare shoulder with the rest of the body hidden in shadows, a motionless silhouette watching her from behind the open blinds, and the diffuse fear that she had been feeling for the past few hours abruptly turned into a feeling of outright terror. She knocked on the door of the pavilion. No one answered. It's me, she said. It's me, let me in. Nothing, no one was answering. She knocked again, harder. Why wasn't I answering, why didn't I want to let her in? Was I there? Marie was panicking, frantically rattling the doorknob. Had something happened to me? Was I there, dead, on the bed, behind the door?

Marie raced back to the front desk and told the lady she was worried that something had happened to me, asked her if she had a master key or a copy of my key. The lady followed her as they hurried through the yard. The lady turned her key in the lock and cracked the door open. The room was a little messy, my white shirt had been thrown on the ground, balled up on the tile floor. The bed, on which a small white waffle-cloth towel had been tossed, was still made. Neither Marie nor the lady had entered the room yet. *C'è qualcuno?* the lady asked. She stepped inside now, cautiously, and looked around. No one was there.

Marie asked the lady if she could wait for me in the room, and she had remained alone in the little pavilion. She had gone through my things with care, had picked my white shirt up off the floor, as well as my undergarments, which were strewn around wherever they'd fallen when I'd undressed before showering. She noticed a few papers and some change on the nightstand, as well as my passport and the large envelope my plane ticket had come in, this containing some travel vouchers, boarding-pass stubs, and taxi receipts, some Chinese money and train tickets, and a ferry pass. She looked closely at the ferry pass, which had been issued by Toremar, Toscana Regionale Marittima S.p.A., for a trip from Piombino to Elba, with today's date.

Marie had removed the towel from the bed in order to lie down. The room was completely silent and still. She had stretched out on her back on the large steel-frame bed, eyes open, lying motionless in the half-light. She was hot. She ended up taking off her boots and then throwing them to the other side of the room, which was no easy task: she had to sit up and move to the edge of the bed and pull hard on each boot, at the risk of popping one of her shoulders out of place. She stretched back out on the bed then, she had no more strength to move. She curled up and slid her hand between her thighs. The heat of the day was pervasive, enveloping her body, she unbuttoned her shirt a little bit, undoing each button one by one, she could feel herself sweating a little, she was waiting for me, she was waiting for me in the room.

Curled up on the bed, she didn't move when I opened the door, her bare stomach showing through her open shirt. The blinds of the sliding-glass door were half-closed, allowing a dim light to shine between their slits and fill the room. I joined Marie on the bed, I hugged her, I felt the stillness of her pain, her silence, as we began, timidly, to caress each other, cautiously, hesitantly, then urgently, all of a sudden, out of control, with a crazy spark in her eyes and the pangs of desire growing stronger and stronger, she reached for my penis, gripped it firmly with her hand, unzipping my pants and kissing it aggressively, with a certain wildness, jerking me off roughly, with a fierce determination, tenaciously, her lips sealed tightly around it now, almost as though she wanted to hurt me, then she curled up against my legs and started to run her tongue all around my penis, not with her usual tenderness or sweetness, but unrestrained, sloppy, as if forcing herself, despite her disgust, to engage in some forbidden act, but then stopping just as abruptly, not insisting, leaving me flat on the bed and lying down on her back so that I could take my own turn, removing her pants, sliding them down her thighs, with the same clumsy impatience, the same lack of tenderness, and I noticed that she wasn't wearing anything underneath her pants, that she didn't have any panties on, her vagina was uncovered before me, and she grabbed my hand and pulled me up toward her. I loved her and I knew I couldn't do anything for her, that it was impossible for us to love each other right then, to seek or take pleasure in this moment, she knew just as well as I did that we couldn't love each other now, I had gotten on top of her and was squeezing her, kissing her naked body in the half-light, tenderly, caringly, I stroked her face to calm her, I was running my tongue up her stomach and around her breasts, I wasn't sure if she had swam today, her skin had a slight seawater taste, a light taste of sweat and coastal shrubs, of heat and salt, her stomach was soft, her thighs were hot, smooth, burning, she was quivering, I was kissing her vagina with my tongue, the inside of her moist and surprisingly cool vagina, which tasted a little bit like iodine, like the sea, I was gently squeezing her hips, I had closed my eyes and I continued to kiss her vagina with my tongue, when, in I don't know what kind of act of impatience or exasperation, of despair or suffocation—or in the sudden and definitive realization that it was impossible for us to love each other right then—abruptly lifting up her pelvis to break away, she pushed me back with a twisting and thrusting movement of her body, giving me, with all her strength, so as to knock me back, a punch in the face with her pussy.

She didn't say a word, didn't give any explanation, she turned over on her side and buried her face in the pillow. I left her alone there, I'd stepped out of the room, walked through the blinds to get some fresh air out on the terrace, barefoot, pants unbuttoned, shirt open, I had sat down on a plastic chair, cracked and wobbly, which was placed next to a white patio table by the small vegetable garden. We hadn't said a word to each other, she remained silent back in the room. She was alone with her pain and I was alone with mine. My love for her had only gotten stronger during this whole trip, and, while I had thought the act of mourning would bring us closer together, unite us in grief, I was beginning to realize that it was actually pulling us apart, and that our suffering, instead of becoming appeased, was becoming all the more acute for the both of us. Close to twenty minutes passed in this way, both of us keeping our distance, without moving, without speaking, Marie in the room and me on the terrace with nothing to do, I'd stretched my legs out in the sun and I was looking at them (they created a sort of a sundial). After a little while longer I saw the blinds move and Marie appeared behind me, calmed, transformed, barefoot, shirt unbuttoned, her riding pants pulled back up around her waist, undone, she was coming to smoke a cigarette in the yard. I lifted my head and she smiled at me as if everything were fine. She sat down cross-legged on a single flagstone, began smoking in silence, barefoot, she turned to look at the small vegetable garden, tomatoes, eggplant, basil, planted directly in the ground, and she told me in a soft voice while gently tearing off a leaf of basil with two fingers that the hotel lady had been really nice to her (not like you, she told me, and she playfully poked my knee with her finger as if to punish me for being inconsiderate). Where were you? she asked me, what did you do this afternoon? Nothing, I said. Nothing,

I probably hadn't done anything more than she had—I'd just wandered aimlessly through the streets of Portoferraio.

Around six o'clock Marie wanted to swim. There weren't any nice beaches in Portoferraio, and Marie suggested that we go get her father's old truck, which had been sitting unused for some time now in the lot by a garage behind the new port (her father had bought a new four-wheel drive truck a few months before his death, and had left the old truck in the vacant lot that adjoined the garage). The sun was still out when we left the hotel, a softer and more agreeable sun than in the early afternoon, and we went down the Salita Cosimo dei Medici with Marie carrying the little waffle-cloth towel from the hotel. We crossed through Portoferraio whose streets were now beginning to come alive, a few specialty food stores had opened near the port. We ducked under a slack wire fence outside the garage—only a mild case of breaking and entering—and we walked through the gray vacant lot filled with rocks and gravel at the back of which I recognized her father's old open-bed truck parked in front of a glass building where used cars for sale were on display. Do you want to drive? I asked Marie. No, not especially, she told me, and she handed me the keys. I got in behind the wheel, sinking down in the soft seat with its old springs, the steering wheel was burning hot, the dashboard covered with bits of straw and parking tickets, a half-empty bottle of mineral water was stuck between the seat and the hand brake, there was a bunch of dried herbs on top of the glove compartment, some fennel, some broom, a few tiny branches of rosemary (it was a real herbarium), which Marie, or her father, must have picked a few years earlier. The smell of coastal shrubs, hot plastic, and horse stables filled the truck; I put the keys in the ignition and started it (on the first try), and we drove out of the potholed lot, rolled over the curb to get around the red and white barrier that, theoretically, kept cars from entering and exiting the lot, and we quickly left Portoferraio behind us. We hadn't talked about a precise destination, but I instinctively took the route toward La Rivercina.

We had left the city and were following winding roads in the sun—there was no breeze in the air, not a single wave in the sea. All of nature around us was green and blue, dominated by the blue of the sky and the green of the vegetation, the intense green of the coastal shrubs and the blue of the motionless sea below us, with the parasol-like figures of tall agave plants forming a procession alongside the road. Marie remained silent, she had put the small waffle-cloth towel from the hotel on her lap and was watching the street unfold in front of her. You want me to tell you a *barzelletta*? I asked her. She looked at me and smiled, surprised, put her hand on my shoulder and softly squeezed my arm, appeased, reassured, as if she had finally found me after a long absence, an eclipse, a temporary lapse in my personality. But this only lasted a second. The sun came out as we turned a corner and its violent orange glare blinded me through the windshield. I squinted my eyes and asked Marie to lend me her sunglasses. She took them off and tried to put them on me herself, in what could have been a kind gesture, which even began as a kind gesture, but which, like all the kind gestures we had attempted today, ended in confusion and awkwardness (since, finding that my face wasn't as flat as she'd anticipated, irritated by my passivity, and then fed up with herself for not being able to put them on right, she ended up shoving the glasses on me crookedly, almost stabbing me in the eye with the frames)—as if, from now on, we would only be able to be together, and to love each other, in discomfort and impatience.

La Rivercina was located in the mining region of Rio nell'Elba. I'd always been aware of the abandoned iron mines on the side of the road to the estate, but I'd never, until today, been so struck by the funereal tone that the disused mines had given to their desolate surroundings, red scars slashing through the heart of the coastal shrubs, open wounds, long rosewood-colored cuts smoldering in the sun, conveying a forlorn kind of beauty. I was driving slowly down windy roads while observing the flayed hillside whose seaside slopes, marked by an absence of vegetation, were filled with iron ore. A wraithlike sand path led down to the beach where the mine's old shacks had been abandoned, roofless, windows broken, surrounded by mining carts tipped over on their sides and iron sheds, all along a coast of iron oxide and a sea of oil, covered in black, a sea of black oil. I had turned off the road a little farther on, onto more of a trail than a road, a dirt path, and I drove as slowly as possible, which didn't prevent us from being flung around inside the truck at each new bump or hole, Marie bracing herself against the glove compartment for support. I drove over an abandoned bridge that straddled a dry riverbed of rocks and pebbles and went up another dusty trail for about a hundred meters more before parking on a cliff towering above the sea. From there a steep path led down to a little beach cove that we were familiar with. No other cars were parked there that night (at times, in the summer, there would be up to four or five, but never more than that, this spot was a well-kept secret).

Marie led the way down the path, descending rather quickly through broom and asphodels, carrying the little waffle-cloth towel from the hotel over her shoulder. At the foot of the path, hidden among brush and wild olive trees, were the ruins of an abandoned chapel, roofless, invaded by vegetation. We walked around the weathered walls of the chapel for a bit, along the cliff sides and giant rocks, before coming out at a tiny shingle beach, which had no vegetation other than a few tall cattails and helianthemums growing around the edge of a small mosquito-infested pool of water at the foot of the cliff. Marie sat down on the shingles and took off her riding boots (I had to help her because they stuck to her legs). Free of her boots, she immediately went to put her feet in the water, while I took off my shirt and sat comfortably on the shore. Marie ambled barefoot along the shoreline, walking back and forth, she wanted to roll up her pant legs so that they wouldn't get wet, but, losing patience rather quickly, she came back over to where I was sitting to take her pants off completely, then walked again to the shoreline, legs and ass fully exposed, wearing nothing more than an unbuttoned shirt that barely reached her hips.

The sea was clear, and the sun had dropped low in the sky, the horizon was nothing more than a streak of red-orange embers on the point of dying out on the surface of the sea. Marie walked back over to me, grabbed me by the hand, and pulled me up onto the beach, and I took her in my arms without saying a word, pulling her body close to mine, squeezing her, calming her with my embrace. Standing still, I felt her warm body in my arms, and I looked at her intently—I was also sad, I was suffering too, could she understand that? We looked into each other's eyes and we began swaying back and forth, I was rocking her slowly in my arms, making her sway with me on the shingle beach, unspeaking, our two bodies had become one, half nude, half dressed, her bare legs moved under my bare torso as if they were attached, while the sides of her shirt flapped around the waist of my pants. We were dancing in place, very slowly, our bodies entwined, and we began shuffling toward the shoreline, both of us stumbling over the shingles, sometimes slipping slightly on small, sharp pebbles, dancing, approaching the sea, stepping into the darker, flattened areas of sand where the dying waves reached their end, we were dancing in the silence of a deserted cove at the foot of a mountain.

Marie had taken off her shirt and headed to the water to swim. I sat back down on the beach and she splashed around in the water in front of me, looking at me, smiling at me, her hands against the shallow seabed, almost motionless, hair wet, letting seawater enter her mouth and spitting it back out, cheeks swollen, making small bubbles. Get in, she told me. I smiled at her but didn't stand up. Come on, she repeated, then she swam off without insisting, swimming the breaststroke out in the open sea, switching to a front crawl, with smooth movements of her arms, very slow, regular, each arm moving individually, lifting toward the sky and descending back down into the sea with a slightly lopsided rhythm. She swam away from the shore and began to swim parallel to the rocky cliff of the mountain, then stopped and started floating on her back, doing the backstroke a few meters, kicking her legs, the back of her head in the water. She was about a dozen meters from shore, and she told me she was going to swim to the next cove, which was just around the base of the mountain. Meet me on the other side, she yelled to me from a distance, take the trail and meet me there with my stuff and the towel—and, without waiting for me to respond, she swam off into the open sea.

I had watched Marie swim slowly off in the sea, she had gone around the great rocky cliff of the mountain and left my view. I had stayed a few more minutes sitting on the beach, then I gathered her things in my arms, her shirt and her riding boots, which were floppy and light when not on her legs, and, placing the little bath towel on top of the bundle, I headed toward the trail to go meet up with her. I struggled back up the trail, shirtless, Marie's belongings in my arms, beginning to sweat as I climbed the cliff, dust and plant leaves sticking to my chest, which was glistening with sweat, I was completely drenched about halfway up even though the sun had practically disappeared behind the mountain. I took wide steps through the coastal shrubs, slipping on rocks, my shoes sliding on the loose dirt, my arms scratched by the brush, by the prickly branches of the bramble—covered with a glaze of beautiful golden light from what remained of the sun—though unmolested by the small-scale activity of local insects. Having reached the top of the incline, I passed by the old truck without stopping and quickly crossed the cliff top, stopping at the edge before the immense drop. I leaned over the abyss to try to spot Marie in the sea below, but there wasn't a single human trace in the sea, the water was silent, black, and still, darkened by the shadow of the steep slope.

I began my way down the brush-filled trail on the other side of the cliff, leading down to the cove where I was supposed to meet Marie. I was still rushing, trying to get there ahead of her and put my growing worry to rest, the first pangs of a panic attack, making my heart race, hurrying through the trail to be with her again and reassure myself, be reassured definitively, rushing so as not to think, not wanting to think, refusing to think, trying to get the idea out of my head, the idea that had formed only after Marie swam away, the idea that hadn't occurred to me while watching her in the water, that hadn't occurred to me before we arrived, when she'd asked me in Portoferraio if I wanted to go swimming, that hadn't made its appearance until a few minutes ago, I'd simply never made the connection until now that her father had drowned, that he'd had his heart attack in the sea, maybe even here, in the same cove, not even three days ago, certainly in a cove somewhere near La Rivercina and maybe even here, exactly where Marie was swimming now, since these were *our* coves, since these were the coves we always went to every time we came to La Rivercina, I'd made the obvious and terrifying connection at last, and I made it all at once, running down the trail, now that the light was fading, now that the sun had set, now that night was falling, now that the path was dark and the coastal shrubs obscured by shadows, dense, prickly, and I was only able to make out the silhouette of some heather being shaken by the breeze in the glowing blue darkness of the thicket. I was running shirtless down the path with Marie's things in my arms, holding her riding pants, bra, and white shirt tight against my chest, her boots somehow incorporated into the bundle, barely hanging on, and I was stumbling over the holes in the path, my feet slipping over a scree of rocks, the soles of my shoes, tractionless, causing me to slide, with no way to slow myself down, finding no support, nowhere to regain my footing, twisting my ankles, even falling on my knee once, my elbow slamming against the hard ground, causing Marie's things to spill out onto the path, stopping to pick them back up, crouching, elbow aching, picking up her dirt-covered pants, her shirt sticking to the viscous leaves of a cistus flower, grabbing the boots and starting back down the path, leaving the bath towel behind, stuck to the thorny branches of a bush, pursuing the trail, limping due to my fall, and, dragging my leg, arriving at the tiny deserted cove.

I ran toward the sea, I ran down the rugged coastline as far as possible, climbing rock after rock to scout the horizon. I stood there, looking out at the sea, shoes soaked and now absorbing even more water on the giant, slippery rocks, but I couldn't see Marie on the horizon, and I understood then what it meant to be abandoned, I understood how Marie must have felt when I'd disappeared that afternoon, when I'd left her for several hours without word, I understood her despair, her helplessness, her unrelenting anxiety. I looked at the dark sea in front of me, at the waves breaking against the rocks, waiting impatiently for Marie to reappear, and I thought that maybe she was just about to arrive and that any moment now I would see her emerge from behind the rocky headland whose features were becoming less distinct in the darkness. Night had fallen. I couldn't wait any longer, I had to do something, I took off my shoes and went after her, waded into the sea. I waded in until the water reached mid-thigh, walking as long as my feet could touch ground, the water now reaching my stomach, and then I leaned forward and dove in. I was swimming in the black water, heavy, endless, dark, I had just left the cove and was still swimming parallel to the coast, I was swimming in the motionless shadow cast by the immense cliff wall, leaving the cove behind me in the silence of the night, my fear growing and growing the more I let the shore disappear from view, the more I entered into the vastness of the sea. I could feel the abyssal depths and various levels of seabed beneath me, the color of the water was turning from blue to purple, with oily patches, black and dense, impenetrable. I opened my eyes underwater and I saw a blurry world of shadows, uneven plains, trenches, a hollow reflection of the looming mountainside above.

The seawater was becoming thicker, it felt more immense the further I swam out, as though it was carrying me, as though I was being borne along by the swell of the sea, vast and undulant, there were a few small eddies on the surface of the water, but these on rising waves, giant swells that collapsed into tiny ripples, leaving swirls of white foam behind them when they broke. I couldn't have swam for more than fifty meters, a hundred meters at most, when I caught sight of a little rock in the distance, a small bobbing rock around which foam and white water were bubbling, unless it was the head of a swimmer, Marie's head, emerging from the darkness about a hundred meters away. I raised my hand and started waving my arm in the night, I called out to her and I began swimming as fast as I could, I looked up again, I was convinced now that it had to be a swimmer's head and not a piece of wreckage or deadwood or a buoy. But Marie didn't know that I was coming toward her, she didn't see me and continued to swim at her normal pace, occasionally lifting her head to take a breath. I was still swimming toward her, I had recognized her now, I was certain, I couldn't make out her face but I recognized her figure and the way she swam. I stopped in the water and waved my arm, I was calling out to her in the night when she finally saw me. We swam toward each other, both of us out of strength now, I could make out her face in the darkness, disappearing and reappearing beneath the waves, her cheeks pale, her face hardly recognizable, cold, stiff, exhausted, marked by an expression of determination, as though she'd been struggling, a look of resolve, of fatigue, of agony, of shock. And, Marie, who hadn't cried the entire day, who'd affected a cold, strong, and distant attitude throughout, who'd kept her composure in spite of her pain, remaining poised, even stubborn, despite her deep sorrow since first hearing about her father's death, Marie who hadn't cried watching her father's burial, who hadn't cried when we finally met at the hotel, waited until there was no space separating us, she waited until she had finally reached me, until she could put her hand on my shoulder, to burst into tears, kissing and hitting me at the same time, wrapping her arms around me, shouting insults at me in the night, shaken by sobs that the sea immediately absorbed into its own brackish body while bubbles of white foam swirled around us, Marie, without strength, immobile in my arms, no longer moving, no longer swimming, just floating in my arms as I stroked her face, squeezing her cold wet body against mine, her legs twisting around my waist, Marie cried tenderly in my arms, and I wiped away her tears with my hand, kissing her, running my hand through her hair and over her cheeks, licking her tears away with my tongue and kissing her, she was letting herself go, I was kissing and collecting her tears with my lips, I could taste the saltwater on my tongue, I had seawater in my eyes, and Marie cried in my arms as I continued to kiss her, she cried in the sea.

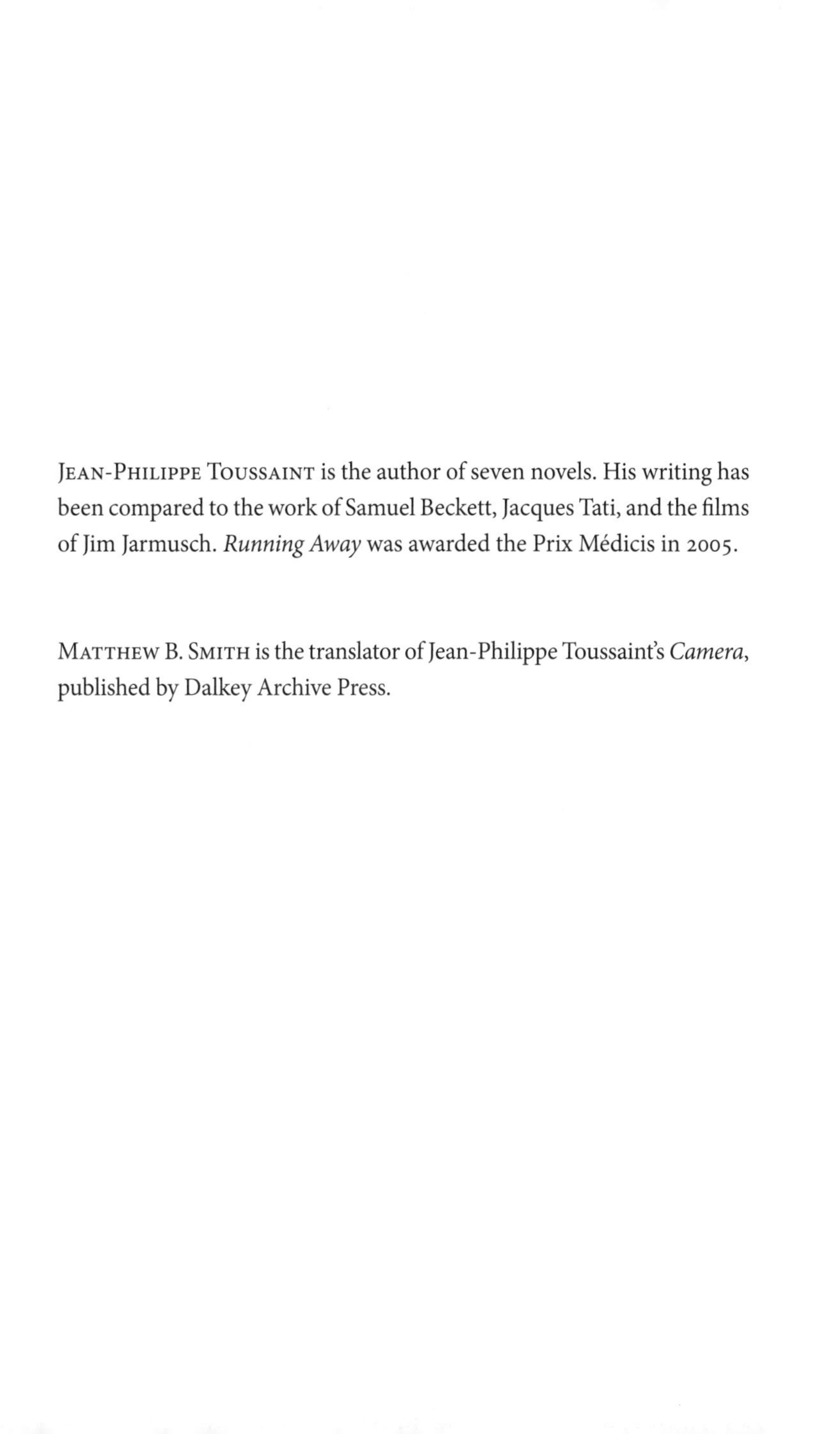

JEAN-PHILIPPE TOUSSAINT is the author of seven novels. His writing has been compared to the work of Samuel Beckett, Jacques Tati, and the films of Jim Jarmusch. *Running Away* was awarded the Prix Médicis in 2005.

MATTHEW B. SMITH is the translator of Jean-Philippe Toussaint's *Camera*, published by Dalkey Archive Press.

SELECTED DALKEY ARCHIVE PAPERBACKS

Petros Abatzoglou, *What Does Mrs. Freeman Want?*
Michal Ajvaz, *The Other City.*
Pierre Albert-Birot, *Grabinoulor.*
Yuz Aleshkovsky, *Kangaroo.*
Felipe Alfau, *Chromos.*
Locos.
Ivan Ângelo, *The Celebration.*
The Tower of Glass.
David Antin, *Talking.*
António Lobo Antunes, *Knowledge of Hell.*
Alain Arias-Misson, *Theatre of Incest.*
John Ashbery and James Schuyler, *A Nest of Ninnies.*
Heimrad Bäcker, *transcript.*
Djuna Barnes, *Ladies Almanack.*
Ryder.
John Barth, *LETTERS.*
Sabbatical.
Donald Barthelme, *The King.*
Paradise.
Svetislav Basara, *Chinese Letter.*
Mark Binelli, *Sacco and Vanzetti Must Die!*
Andrei Bitov, *Pushkin House.*
Louis Paul Boon, *Chapel Road.*
My Little War.
Summer in Termuren.
Roger Boylan, *Killoyle.*
Ignácio de Loyola Brandão, *Anonymous Celebrity.*
Teeth under the Sun.
Zero.
Bonnie Bremser, *Troia: Mexican Memoirs.*
Christine Brooke-Rose, *Amalgamemnon.*
Brigid Brophy, *In Transit.*
Meredith Brosnan, *Mr. Dynamite.*
Gerald L. Bruns, *Modern Poetry and the Idea of Language.*
Evgeny Bunimovich and J. Kates, eds., *Contemporary Russian Poetry: An Anthology.*
Gabrielle Burton, *Heartbreak Hotel.*
Michel Butor, *Degrees.*
Mobile.
Portrait of the Artist as a Young Ape.
G. Cabrera Infante, *Infante's Inferno.*
Three Trapped Tigers.
Julieta Campos, *The Fear of Losing Eurydice.*
Anne Carson, *Eros the Bittersweet.*
Camilo José Cela, *Christ versus Arizona.*
The Family of Pascual Duarte.
The Hive.
Louis-Ferdinand Céline, *Castle to Castle.*
Conversations with Professor Y.
London Bridge.
Normance.
North.
Rigadoon.
Hugo Charteris, *The Tide Is Right.*
Jerome Charyn, *The Tar Baby.*
Marc Cholodenko, *Mordechai Schamz.*
Emily Holmes Coleman, *The Shutter of Snow.*
Robert Coover, *A Night at the Movies.*
Stanley Crawford, *Log of the S.S. The Mrs Unguentine.*
Some Instructions to My Wife.
Robert Creeley, *Collected Prose.*
René Crevel, *Putting My Foot in It.*
Ralph Cusack, *Cadenza.*
Susan Daitch, *L.C.*
Storytown.
Nicholas Delbanco, *The Count of Concord.*
Nigel Dennis, *Cards of Identity.*
Peter Dimock, *A Short Rhetoric for Leaving the Family.*
Ariel Dorfman, *Konfidenz.*
Coleman Dowell, *The Houses of Children.*
Island People.
Too Much Flesh and Jabez.
Arkadii Dragomoshchenko, *Dust.*
Rikki Ducornet, *The Complete Butcher's Tales.*
The Fountains of Neptune.
The Jade Cabinet.
The One Marvelous Thing.
Phosphor in Dreamland.
The Stain.
The Word "Desire."
William Eastlake, *The Bamboo Bed.*
Castle Keep.
Lyric of the Circle Heart.
Jean Echenoz, *Chopin's Move.*
Stanley Elkin, *A Bad Man.*
Boswell: A Modern Comedy.
Criers and Kibitzers, Kibitzers and Criers.
The Dick Gibson Show.
The Franchiser.
George Mills.
The Living End.
The MacGuffin.
The Magic Kingdom.
Mrs. Ted Bliss.
The Rabbi of Lud.
Van Gogh's Room at Arles.
Annie Ernaux, *Cleaned Out.*
Lauren Fairbanks, *Muzzle Thyself.*
Sister Carrie.
Juan Filloy, *Op Oloop.*
Leslie A. Fiedler, *Love and Death in the American Novel.*
Gustave Flaubert, *Bouvard and Pécuchet.*
Kass Fleisher, *Talking out of School.*
Ford Madox Ford, *The March of Literature.*
Jon Fosse, *Melancholy.*
Max Frisch, *I'm Not Stiller.*
Man in the Holocene.
Carlos Fuentes, *Christopher Unborn.*
Distant Relations.
Terra Nostra.
Where the Air Is Clear.
Janice Galloway, *Foreign Parts.*
The Trick Is to Keep Breathing.
William H. Gass, *Cartesian Sonata and Other Novellas.*
Finding a Form.
A Temple of Texts.
The Tunnel.
Willie Masters' Lonesome Wife.
Gérard Gavarry, *Hoppla! 1 2 3.*
Etienne Gilson, *The Arts of the Beautiful.*
Forms and Substances in the Arts.
C. S. Giscombe, *Giscome Road.*
Here.
Prairie Style.
Douglas Glover, *Bad News of the Heart.*
The Enamoured Knight.
Witold Gombrowicz, *A Kind of Testament.*
Karen Elizabeth Gordon, *The Red Shoes.*
Georgi Gospodinov, *Natural Novel.*
Juan Goytisolo, *Count Julian.*
Juan the Landless.
Makbara.
Marks of Identity.
Patrick Grainville, *The Cave of Heaven.*
Henry Green, *Back.*
Blindness.
Concluding.
Doting.
Nothing.
Jiří Gruša, *The Questionnaire.*
Gabriel Gudding, *Rhode Island Notebook.*
John Hawkes, *Whistlejacket.*
Aleksandar Hemon, ed., *Best European Fiction 2010.*
Aidan Higgins, *A Bestiary.*
Balcony of Europe.
Bornholm Night-Ferry.
Darkling Plain: Texts for the Air.
Flotsam and Jetsam.
Langrishe, Go Down.
Scenes from a Receding Past.
Windy Arbours.
Aldous Huxley, *Antic Hay.*
Crome Yellow.
Point Counter Point.
Those Barren Leaves.
Time Must Have a Stop.
Mikhail Iossel and Jeff Parker, eds., *Amerika: Contemporary Russians View the United States.*
Gert Jonke, *Geometric Regional Novel.*
Homage to Czerny.
The System of Vienna.
Jacques Jouet, *Mountain R.*
Savage.
Charles Juliet, *Conversations with Samuel Beckett and Bram van Velde.*
Mieko Kanai, *The Word Book.*
Hugh Kenner, *The Counterfeiters.*
Flaubert, Joyce and Beckett: The Stoic Comedians.
Joyce's Voices.
Danilo Kiš, *Garden, Ashes.*
A Tomb for Boris Davidovich.
Anita Konkka, *A Fool's Paradise.*
George Konrád, *The City Builder.*
Tadeusz Konwicki, *A Minor Apocalypse.*
The Polish Complex.
Menis Koumandareas, *Koula.*
Elaine Kraf, *The Princess of 72nd Street.*
Jim Krusoe, *Iceland.*
Ewa Kuryluk, *Century 21.*
Eric Laurrent, *Do Not Touch.*
Violette Leduc, *La Bâtarde.*
Suzanne Jill Levine, *The Subversive Scribe: Translating Latin American Fiction.*
Deborah Levy, *Billy and Girl.*
Pillow Talk in Europe and Other Places.
José Lezama Lima, *Paradiso.*
Rosa Liksom, *Dark Paradise.*
Osman Lins, *Avalovara.*
The Queen of the Prisons of Greece.
Alf Mac Lochlainn, *The Corpus in the Library.*
Out of Focus.
Ron Loewinsohn, *Magnetic Field(s).*
Brian Lynch, *The Winner of Sorrow.*
D. Keith Mano, *Take Five.*
Micheline Aharonian Marcom, *The Mirror in the Well.*
Ben Marcus, *The Age of Wire and String.*
Wallace Markfield, *Teitlebaum's Window.*
To an Early Grave.
David Markson, *Reader's Block.*
Springer's Progress.
Wittgenstein's Mistress.
Carole Maso, *AVA.*

FOR A FULL LIST OF PUBLICATIONS, VISIT:
www.dalkeyarchive.com

SELECTED DALKEY ARCHIVE PAPERBACKS

Ladislav Matejka and Krystyna Pomorska, eds.,
Readings in Russian Poetics: Formalist and Structuralist Views.
Harry Mathews,
The Case of the Persevering Maltese: Collected Essays.
Cigarettes.
The Conversions.
The Human Country: New and Collected Stories.
The Journalist.
My Life in CIA.
Singular Pleasures.
The Sinking of the Odradek Stadium.
Tlooth.
20 Lines a Day.
Robert L. McLaughlin, ed., *Innovations: An Anthology of Modern & Contemporary Fiction.*
Herman Melville, *The Confidence-Man.*
Amanda Michalopoulou, *I'd Like.*
Steven Millhauser, *The Barnum Museum.*
In the Penny Arcade.
Ralph J. Mills, Jr., *Essays on Poetry.*
Momus, *The Book of Jokes.*
Christine Montalbetti, *Western.*
Olive Moore, *Spleen.*
Nicholas Mosley, *Accident.*
Assassins.
Catastrophe Practice.
Children of Darkness and Light.
Experience and Religion.
God's Hazard.
The Hesperides Tree.
Hopeful Monsters.
Imago Bird.
Impossible Object.
Inventing God.
Judith.
Look at the Dark.
Natalie Natalia.
Paradoxes of Peace.
Serpent.
Time at War.
The Uses of Slime Mould: Essays of Four Decades.
Warren Motte,
Fables of the Novel: French Fiction since 1990.
Fiction Now: The French Novel in the 21st Century.
Oulipo: A Primer of Potential Literature.
Yves Navarre, *Our Share of Time.*
Sweet Tooth.
Dorothy Nelson, *In Night's City.*
Tar and Feathers.
Wilfrido D. Nolledo, *But for the Lovers.*
Flann O'Brien, *At Swim-Two-Birds.*
At War.
The Best of Myles.
The Dalkey Archive.
Further Cuttings.
The Hard Life.
The Poor Mouth.
The Third Policeman.
Claude Ollier, *The Mise-en-Scène.*
Patrik Ouředník, *Europeana.*
Fernando del Paso, *News from the Empire.*
Palinuro of Mexico.
Robert Pinget, *The Inquisitory.*
Mahu or The Material.
Trio.
Manuel Puig, *Betrayed by Rita Hayworth.*
Heartbreak Tango.
Raymond Queneau, *The Last Days.*
Odile.
Pierrot Mon Ami.
Saint Glinglin.
Ann Quin, *Berg.*
Passages.
Three.
Tripticks.
Ishmael Reed, *The Free-Lance Pallbearers.*
The Last Days of Louisiana Red.
The Plays.
Reckless Eyeballing.
The Terrible Threes.
The Terrible Twos.
Yellow Back Radio Broke-Down.
Jean Ricardou, *Place Names.*
Rainer Maria Rilke,
The Notebooks of Malte Laurids Brigge.
Julián Ríos, *Larva: A Midsummer Night's Babel.*
Poundemonium.
Augusto Roa Bastos, *I the Supreme.*
Olivier Rolin, *Hotel Crystal.*
Jacques Roubaud, *The Form of a City Changes Faster, Alas, Than the Human Heart.*
The Great Fire of London.
Hortense in Exile.
Hortense Is Abducted.
The Loop.
The Plurality of Worlds of Lewis.
The Princess Hoppy.
Some Thing Black.
Leon S. Roudiez, *French Fiction Revisited.*
Vedrana Rudan, *Night.*
Stig Sæterbakken, *Siamese.*
Lydie Salvayre, *The Company of Ghosts.*
Everyday Life.
The Lecture.
Portrait of the Writer as a Domesticated Animal.
The Power of Flies.
Luis Rafael Sánchez, *Macho Camacho's Beat.*
Severo Sarduy, *Cobra & Maitreya.*
Nathalie Sarraute, *Do You Hear Them?*
Martereau.
The Planetarium.
Arno Schmidt, *Collected Stories.*
Nobodaddy's Children.
Christine Schutt, *Nightwork.*
Gail Scott, *My Paris.*
Damion Searls, *What We Were Doing and Where We Were Going.*
June Akers Seese,
Is This What Other Women Feel Too?
What Waiting Really Means.
Bernard Share, *Inish.*
Transit.
Aurelie Sheehan, *Jack Kerouac Is Pregnant.*
Viktor Shklovsky, *Knight's Move.*
A Sentimental Journey: Memoirs 1917–1922.
Energy of Delusion: A Book on Plot.
Literature and Cinematography.
Theory of Prose.
Third Factory.
Zoo, or Letters Not about Love.
Josef Škvorecký, *The Engineer of Human Souls.*
Claude Simon, *The Invitation.*
Gilbert Sorrentino, *Aberration of Starlight.*
Blue Pastoral.
Crystal Vision.
Imaginative Qualities of Actual Things.
Mulligan Stew.
Pack of Lies.
Red the Fiend.
The Sky Changes.
Something Said.
Splendide-Hôtel.
Steelwork.
Under the Shadow.
W. M. Spackman, *The Complete Fiction.*
Andrzej Stasiuk, *Fado.*
Gertrude Stein, *Lucy Church Amiably.*
The Making of Americans.
A Novel of Thank You.
Piotr Szewc, *Annihilation.*
Gonçalo M. Tavares, *Jerusalem.*
Lucian Dan Teodorovici, *Our Circus Presents . . . .*
Stefan Themerson, *Hobson's Island.*
The Mystery of the Sardine.
Tom Harris.
Jean-Philippe Toussaint, *The Bathroom.*
Camera.
Monsieur.
Running Away.
Television.
Dumitru Tsepeneag, *Pigeon Post.*
The Necessary Marriage.
Vain Art of the Fugue.
Esther Tusquets, *Stranded.*
Dubravka Ugresic, *Lend Me Your Character.*
Thank You for Not Reading.
Mati Unt, *Brecht at Night*
Diary of a Blood Donor.
Things in the Night.
Álvaro Uribe and Olivia Sears, eds.,
The Best of Contemporary Mexican Fiction.
Eloy Urroz, *The Obstacles.*
Luisa Valenzuela, *He Who Searches.*
Paul Verhaeghen, *Omega Minor.*
Marja-Liisa Vartio, *The Parson's Widow.*
Boris Vian, *Heartsnatcher.*
Ornela Vorpsi, *The Country Where No One Ever Dies.*
Austryn Wainhouse, *Hedyphagetica.*
Paul West, *Words for a Deaf Daughter & Gala.*
Curtis White, *America's Magic Mountain.*
The Idea of Home.
Memories of My Father Watching TV.
Monstrous Possibility: An Invitation to Literary Politics.
Requiem.
Diane Williams, *Excitability: Selected Stories.*
Romancer Erector.
Douglas Woolf, *Wall to Wall.*
Ya! & John-Juan.
Jay Wright, *Polynomials and Pollen.*
The Presentable Art of Reading Absence.
Philip Wylie, *Generation of Vipers.*
Marguerite Young, *Angel in the Forest.*
Miss MacIntosh, My Darling.
REYoung, *Unbabbling.*
Zoran Živković, *Hidden Camera.*
Louis Zukofsky, *Collected Fiction.*
Scott Zwiren, *God Head.*

FOR A FULL LIST OF PUBLICATIONS, VISIT:
www.dalkeyarchive.com